MONTANA MAVERICKS

Welcome to Big Sky Country, home of the Montana Mavericks! Where free-spirited men and women discover love on the range.

THE TENACITY SOCIAL CLUB

In rough-and-tumble Tenacity, it seems everyone already knows everyone else—*and* their business. Finding someone new to date can be a struggle. But what if your perfect match is already written in the stars? Pull up a barstool and open your heart, because you never know who you might meet at the Social Club!

When you've found your soulmate, why would you deny it? Lucy Bernard knows from the start that Noah Trent is the man for her. The rancher keeps pushing her away, though, insisting she's too young to be saddled with three little kids. He's afraid history will repeat itself; she's afraid she's going to lose her perfect cowboy before he even gives them a chance...

Dear Reader,

Welcome to Tenacity! I've loved my time in this small, hardworking Montana town. The people are real, trustworthy and not afraid to get their hands dirty to help each other. This story spoke to me a lot because as an introverted reader growing up, I was happier at home, reading or writing. Which made me different from pretty much everyone else around me, and I often felt as though I should get out to the big city and make more of myself. Lucy, in this story, did just that. And was brave enough to admit that she wanted to live in the small town she'd grown up in, surrounded by the people she'd known all her life. I celebrated that choice with her!

And Noah, well, loving him is just a given. Raising three small boys, potty training them, all alone, and maintaining patience while doing so—the man is most definitely hero material. He's a rancher, used to tough work, and yet these three little guys manage to challenge him at every turn.

I hope you enjoy your time here as much as I have! The good news is, you get to return again and again. This town, these people...we're just getting started!

Tara Taylor Quinn

MAVERICK'S FULL HOUSE

TARA TAYLOR QUINN

MONTANA MAVERICKS

Special thanks and acknowledgment are given to
Tara Taylor Quinn for her contribution to the
Montana Mavericks: The Tenacity Social Club miniseries.

MONTANA MAVERICKS

ISBN-13: 978-1-335-14322-8

Maverick's Full House

Copyright © 2025 by Harlequin Enterprises ULC

Harlequin Enterprises ULC
22 Adelaide St. West, 41st Floor
Toronto, Ontario M5H 4E3, Canada
www.Harlequin.com

Printed in Lithuania

MIX
Paper | Supporting
responsible forestry
FSC® C021394

Recycling programs
for this product may
not exist in your area.

A *USA TODAY* bestselling author of over one hundred novels in twenty languages, **Tara Taylor Quinn** has sold more than seven million copies. Known for her intense emotional fiction, Ms. Quinn's novels have received critical acclaim in the UK and most recently from Harvard. She is the recipient of the Readers' Choice Award and has appeared often on local and national TV, including *CBS Sunday Morning*. For TTQ offers, news and contests, visit tarataylorquinn.com!

Visit the Author Profile page
at Harlequin.com for more titles.

For Timothy: My rugged hero, and the most gentle, patient and playful man I know when it comes to the littles. You have my heart forever.

Chapter One

Three little guys, toddler bodies wiggling, stood in a row, facing three urinals carefully home-manufactured to be just the right height. Henry, almost two years old, and the middle one by four minutes on one side and three on the other, nudged Gavin, the baby. Charlie, the oldest by three minutes, stood at attention. Heart over-flowing with love, their dad, Noah Trent, moved his cowboy boots one step at a time down the line, starting with Gavin, pulling away disposable overnight diapers where his little men stood.

Rolling two of the saturated diapers in the third, he said, "Okay, guys, go pee pee." And secured the nightly trash in his hand with the tabs on number three, before dropping them in the lidded and lined can there for that purpose.

"Pee pee," Charlie said, touching his little nubbin.

Henry nudged Gavin again—who ignored him—as Henry stared in his brother's bowl just as Gavin dripped a couple of drops inside. Henry dove for them, and Noah grabbed the pudgy little hands before they reached their target, hauling the naked-bottomed child up under one arm saying, "That's my man, Gavin!! See, boys, what

Gavin did. Pee pee. We do it here, just like that." Charlie, leaning over to look, let go with a stream down his leg and onto the floor.

Grabbing up son number one before he could step in his own puddle, Noah held the two wriggling bodies against him—their legs dangling together—with one arm as he reached down with his free hand to grab up Gavin, the runt of the group. And made a beeline for the already filled bathtub, with the three-inch-deep safety mat securely mounted to the bottom. And foam on the walls around it, too.

From there, he grabbed the paper towels and disinfecting cleaner from under the sink, expertly eliminated the puddle from the floor and deposited the remains in the diaper pail. And tended to Gavin's few drops, too. He'd started training way early. Didn't expect results yet. The boys most likely didn't even have the ability to control output. But when they came into their own, they'd know exactly what to do and where.

Same reason they'd all been up in the saddle—on a stationary wooden saddle horse with the legs cut off—since the time they could sit up.

Glancing at the clock, Noah bent down on one knee, was reaching for the sponge and tearless soap when Charlie raised both arms in the air and splashed his hands down into the water. His two siblings, in typical fashion, followed suit immediately, soaking the front of Noah's freshly showered and dried closely cropped hair. A strand of it releasing droplets down into his eye.

"Hey, diddy-diddy, who's going to be in trouble if they don't quit making Daddy wet?" he sang in a tune that was a little bit like the alphabet song.

Three pairs of wide blue eyes turned to him, and he dove in on Gavin with the soapy sponge, then Charlie, and finally, Henry. Toys were dispersed, and Noah took five minutes to sit on the closed toilet seat and dry his hair while his triplets played. At least, until a wildly tossed fish conked him in the head, soaking him all over again.

Picking up the fish, Noah stood. "No throwing toys at people or lobbing them out of the tub," he said, and grabbed the first of three stacked towels off the counter beside the toilet and hauled Henry out of the water. He had the squirmy toddler dried and in his pull-up diaper before the first minute was up. And followed quickly with the other two.

He glanced at the clock again.

And then nodded. He'd done it. Met his goal. A minute per little man. Washing. One minute each. And then dried and diapered. Also a minute each. Letting the water out of the tub, he was all full of congratulating himself, and hanging little hooded towels, until he heard a scream—a mad one—come from the nursery next door, followed by a wailing cry emitted by a different set of lungs. Charlie and Henry.

Dropping the last towel, Noah bolted.

Sitting behind the colorfully decorated reception counter on morning desk duty, marketing specialist Lucy Bernard yearned to be in the back with the kiddos. Working at Little Cowpokes Daycare Center wasn't just a job to make money. Or a place where she was employed because her mother, Elaina, was one of the two women who ran the business. She was there because being around kids made her happier than most anything else.

If her first priority was the money she could make, she'd still be a junior marketing executive in Bronco. Doing a job she really liked, excelled at, but didn't love.

Not like she loved her hardscrabble but mighty hometown of Tenacity.

The thought had her reaching for the pen and notepad there to take phone messages, and making a list of all of Tenacity's good points—exactly as she would were she taking on a new client and designing a campaign that would grow the company's financial security. Tenacity had been a thriving small town when she'd been little. Until around the time she was in third grade someone had emptied the town's financial coffers. But the money had been found. Surely once it made it through the courts, and the thief had been brought to justice, the town would get its assets back.

Getting excited at the thought of possibly being a part of growing back her town's security, she was so fully focused on her list—that was beginning to resemble a tree with branches—that she jumped when the front door opened.

"Sorry we're later than I'd thought we'd be," a deep male voice said as the owner, head down toward the ground, maneuvered a double-wide stroller over the threshold and through the door. "Had a mandatory time-out we couldn't miss."

The man, a bursting-at-the-seams backpack on his shoulder, looked up and Lucy's internal compass needle shot a full circle. She put it down to standing up too quickly. Noah Trent. Their one no-show. And part of the reason she'd had to sit out front to watch the reception area.

Just in case he showed up, Elaina hadn't wanted him to find no one waiting for him.

Her mother had figured him for having an emergency on the ranch requiring all hands on deck, which would most definitely take precedence to starting his boys in daycare. She'd told Lucy Noah was doing so in order to give his parents a break from watching them.

As Mom had relayed it to Lucy, Olive and Christopher Trent hadn't been all that eager to give up the boys.

Lucy hadn't expected the triplets' father to be delivering them. At least not alone. They pretty much always saw the mothers at Little Cowpokes. Plus, she knew ranching was hard work. And started before the sun was up a lot of the time.

Hurrying from behind the counter to help the father who was far too handsome for her neglected libido, Lucy bent down to occupy the little guy Noah set free, while he was working on the other two.

"What's your name?" she asked the almost two-year-old who stood, big blue eyes staring at her, but not appearing the least bit afraid.

"Diddy," the blond-haired urchin said and then gave Lucy a smile that completely melted her.

Smiling back, she said, "No, you have to be either Charlie, Henry or Gavin." She rattled off the names she'd read on their registration sheet. And noticed the second freed captive hanging back by his father who was working on number three.

Those strong, steady adult male hands…three small,

adorable boys... If Lucy had been chocolate she'd have been a puddle on the floor.

"Chawie," the toddler in front of her said, taking a step forward as he reached for the beads braided into two strands of hair framing her face on either side. "Me Chawie."

"I," said the slightly muffled voice of the man ducked under the canopy of a four-seater wagon-style stroller. "*I'm* Charlie, not me Charlie."

Charlie, not even looking back at his father, seemed oblivious to the mini grammar lesson he'd received as he reached out to touch the line of beads in Lucy's hair.

"I'm Lucy," she said, reaching out to steady the toddler, as she let him explore the moon, star and butterfly beads she'd braided into a small strand of her loosely curled blond hair that morning. His pudgy little fingers touched every one of the shiny plastic pieces. Gently. Almost with reverence. And as Lucy squatted there, watching those young blue eyes study her impromptu morning creation, the baby boy invaded her heart.

He had a herd of two hundred cattle to run, and Noah felt far more capable of doing that than leaving his sons at daycare. With Henry clinging to Noah's leg, Noah lifted Gavin out of the stroller, and up onto his hip, in time to see Charlie lifting fingers that had been in his mouth to the young woman's silky blond hair.

He took a breath, intending to deliver the message that would teach his son that his act was inappropriate, but the air caught in the back of his throat, stifling the words. The young woman's smile—Lucy, he'd heard her tell his son—had distracted him. More so because that grin was directed at his most precocious toddler who'd just gooped up her hair. With no admonition at all.

"Show me the moon," were the words coming out of her mouth. A rush of ridiculous pride shot through him when Charlie immediately touched the moon bead at the top of the one skinny little braid hanging at the side of the woman's face.

And Henry let go of Noah to go stand beside his brother, staring from Lucy's face to the beads. "Uh," Henry added his contribution to the moment, with a point toward the braid.

"You want to show me the star?" Lucy asked the newcomer to the little impromptu party. At Henry's nod, she moved her head close enough for him to do so.

Henry touched the star. And then the butterfly. Maybe because he didn't know the difference. More likely because he'd done as he was told and just wanted to touch all the beads. Henry mostly just went wherever the flow took him. Noah figured the boy walked to the beat of his own drummer.

While the two toddlers reached out to something new, Noah glanced at Gavin. Holding tightly to Noah's arm, Gavin had a finger in his mouth as he watched the scene unfolding in front of them. "You want to see the beads, too?" Noah asked him, and wasn't at all surprised when Gavin's arm around his bicep became a death grip and the little guy hid his face in Noah's chest.

Was it too soon to be foisting the boys off on virtual strangers? Guilt hit him. On both sides. Since the triplets had started walking, his parents had been giving up more and more of their own pursuits. Not just when the boys were with them, but afterward, too, as they were so tired out.

Noah could relate. He was pretty sure he hadn't had a full night's sleep since his sons were born.

But the responsibility was his. Not theirs. He'd made his choices. And as their eldest of four children, he was supposed to be helping to lighten their load, not dump an avalanche on them.

"You got here just in time for juice and then train rides." Lucy's voice rose in volume and in pitch, too, as she quickly approached Noah, lifted Gavin out of his arms and, turning away, said, "You want to be first, Gavin? I'll ride with you!" Then, with a slightly apologetic look thrown over her shoulder at Noah, she looked at the other two, saying, "Follow me, guys, and who gets to go second?" as she pushed through the door leading back to the secured daycare rooms. Noah could still hear her chirping to a seemingly mesmerized—or in shock— Gavin as her voice faded in the distance.

And just like that…he'd done his first daycare drop-off.

Without even getting a goodbye.

Lucy was half-heartedly consuming a late lunch of fresh fruit with a tuna sandwich, once again out front manning the phones, when, not surprisingly, it rang.

Noah Trent. His name had been programmed into Little Cowpokes caller identification the week before, right after he'd filled out all paperwork and paid for the first month of daycare for his triplets. Angela Corey—matriarch of the multiple generation Tenacity Corey ranching family—had met with him that day. Angela ran the daycare with Lucy's mom.

Both women had told her to expect the calls during her lunch break. They'd been coming all day. Pretty much on the hour. Glancing at the clock on the wall as she picked up, Lucy said, "You're fifteen minutes late," in a teasing tone. As though she knew the man as more than a name, a face, in the town where she'd grown up. "I apologize, Mr. Trent," she quickly amended. "I've been pretty much glued to your tribe all morning and feel as though I know you through them."

She wondered why his wife wasn't making any of the first-day check-in calls. Then she reminded herself that he had one, as his answering chuckle did inappropriate things to her womanly insides.

"Call me Noah. And you're politely telling me I'm a little over the top." His deep voice didn't carry a hint of having been offended.

"More like I'm finding your first-day jitters kind of nice." Another truth popped out without her forethought. Usual in her personal life, maybe, but not in her professional one. And to cover, she barreled forth with, "The boys are all doing fine. No tears all day, they ate decent-sized lunches, and, once he was lying between Henry and Charlie on their mats for story time, Gavin let me out of his sight."

"He's the shy one." Four words. And she got a delicious tingle. What in the heck was the matter with her? It wasn't like she was man-hungry. Or even looking for one at the moment. Too many things in her life to get settled first.

Like finding a remote marketing job so she could

have her career and live in quaint little blue-collar Tenacity at the same time.

And even if she was in the market for a mate, Noah Trent would not be it. Not only was the man ten years older than her, he was married!

Which made him off-limits—and maybe safe ground for her womanhood to stay in practice? Just so she didn't forget it was there? Lord knew, there were no eligible men in Tenacity in her decade that she hadn't already tried on, only to find another uncomfortable fit.

Unlike his little Gavin, who'd found his way in in mere seconds.

"He's also pretty good at getting what he needs when he needs it," she said, thinking of the number of times the smallest of the blond-haired, blue-eyed trio had managed to persuade her to pick him up and carry him around, or have him sit on her lap, as they'd made their way through the morning's activities.

"He had a lot of them—needs—starting out," Noah Trent said. And then, as though realizing that he was talking to a working professional, he cleared his throat and said, "I was actually just calling to let someone know that I'm on my way into town to pick them up," leaving her disappointed not to hear more about Gavin's beginnings. "I finished a roundup sooner than I expected this morning, and there's a new litter of kittens in the barn that the boys will want to see."

More like Daddy had made it through the morning, and that was enough for day one, Lucy translated. After all the new activities, toys and kids they'd been exposed to, those little boys needed a nap, and she'd bet her week's earnings that all three would be asleep in their car seats long before they ever made it back to their daddy's barn.

Smiling because no one could see, she told Noah that she'd get his children ready, and rang off.

Telling herself to get a grip.

But didn't manage to diminish the grin at all.

Life in Tenacity had just taken on a new sparkle. In a very wrong place.

Maybe it *was* time for her to spend an evening at the Tenacity Social Club and find someone to date.

Chapter Two

Tension eased out of Noah as soon as he saw his three little men walking out through the door that led to the back of the colorful and artfully decorated childcare facility. Charlie in the lead. Then Henry and Gavin. All speeding up as they saw him, hands outstretched. Grabbing all three at once in a bear hug that felt permanent, Noah figured the experiment for a one and done.

Until Charlie hesitated before crawling into his stroller seat, and turned back toward the young woman, Lucy, who'd checked them in earlier. The petite blonde was standing by the door through which she'd led his boys upon his arrival. Charlie waved. "Bye-bye, MeWoo," he said. His childish command of his language giving the salutation somewhat of an adult feel. Henry, watching his brother, waved, too.

And then Gavin, whom Noah had picked up, squirmed to get down. The smallest of his boys stood with a hand on Noah's leg, waved and then held his arms up to be picked up again.

Such a small thing. A few seconds in a lifetime, and Noah was poleaxed. Gavin, his shy little guy who'd spent more time in a hospital than any child should ever have to, had just asserted himself to reach out to a virtual stranger.

Mouth open, Noah stared at the young woman—who was staring back at him. He blinked, nodded, told her they'd see her tomorrow and, still holding Gavin with one hand, used the other to get the stroller laden with his other two offspring out the door. At which time he stopped to strap in Charlie and Henry for the twenty steps to the SUV he'd purchased the day he'd heard he and Joanna were having triplets. He carried Gavin to the car.

Not at all sure what had just happened.

"Don't even think about it."

Hearing her mother's voice, Lucy spun around. Pretending that she hadn't just been caught staring at the closed door through which Noah Trent and his triplets had just departed—Charlie turning in his stroller to wave at her again as he was pushed through the door.

"Think about what?" she asked, mostly with innocence. The ruminations her mother had so rudely interrupted were merely hopes for the future. That someday Lucy would be married to a homegrown decent man like Noah Trent and have children of her own. The man himself was merely a stand-in. A placeholder. He was married, and she most definitely did not entertain thoughts of an affair. Ever.

Or of breaking up a marriage, either.

"The man's got baggage, Luce. You've got your whole life waiting for you. Job opportunities to explore. A world full of choices. A divorced father with three kids would be the end of all of that."

All of what, exactly, Lucy wasn't sure. But she homed in on the one thing she heard clearly. "He's divorced?"

She hadn't heard that part before. But then, until Noah Trent had walked into Little Cowpokes that morning, she hadn't seen him as anything other than the hundred or three other men in town who were married and raising kids.

"His wife left him when the boys were just six months old," Elaina said, coming around the counter to stand right in front of Lucy.

As though Lucy was still ten or fifteen. Or the young eighteen she'd been when she left Tenacity to attend Montana State University in Billings. She couldn't wait to get away. To escape from beneath her mother's well-intentioned, loving but suffocating overprotectiveness. Being an only child hadn't been a cakewalk.

A bone-deep need for her independence had been largely behind her choice to stay away from home after she graduated, too. To accept the junior marketing executive position she'd been offered in Bronco. She'd been good at it. So good she'd been offered a promotion.

One that she hadn't immediately accepted. Which had been the catalyst that had brought her home. She'd loved the work. But she hadn't been all that happy. She'd missed Tenacity. More, she'd seen herself building a life that didn't fill her heart with joy. Being home did that. Contributing to the town she loved. Getting married. Being a mother of children raised in Tenacity. Those were the things her heart most desired.

And that wasn't something her mother—who saw more opportunities for her only child than she'd had—was going to understand. Which was why she stood there silently. Long enough that Elaina continued on, supporting her point with additional facts. Like the fact that not only did Noah Trent have those boys to contend with on his own, but he was running his own spread at Stargazer Ranch—his family's home for generations. "His life is set in stone, Lucy," Elaina said. "His choices already made. Your own wouldn't be able to flourish. You'd be settling for his."

In the first place, she'd merely found the man unbelievably attractive. And his boys a bit of that joy she hadn't found in the city. She hadn't been thinking about asking him out. Let alone seeing a life with him.

But then...he wasn't married.

Maybe she should ask him out.

"Listen, Lucy, as lovely as Noah seems, there's a reason why his wife left him. That's right," Elaina continued. "He didn't want the divorce. She left him..."

"Hey, you two, kiddos are waking up," Angela Corey, Elaina's attractive Black partner and friend, said as she pushed through the door to the reception area, a one-year-old on her hip.

"Let me take her for you." Lucy reached for the baby Angela held. "I'm on changing duty this afternoon." They took turns with the after-nap duty since the changing room really only fit one person comfortably.

She'd have made the offer even if it hadn't been her turn.

Changing dirty diapers was a party compared to finding a way to shut down her mother's smothering in a way that didn't hurt Elaina's feelings.

Or make her think, for one second, that Lucy didn't adore her.

Because she did.

She was also quite fond of the information her mother had imparted.

Noah Trent was single.

The news opened the door to any number of possibilities.

Due to the way his boys had responded to Little Cowpokes—he preferred to think of the triplets' attachment to Lucy Bernard as more of a generic, being-out-among-other-kids-with-activities-specifically-designed-to-entertain-and-teach-them thing as opposed to an attachment to one of the daycare's employees—Noah felt it necessary to tackle a day two at Little Cowpokes. Just to make sure that he hadn't dreamed up Gavin's acting so completely out of character. Or the unusual reactions of the other two, either. Their minute show of independence from him. Always before, once Noah was around, the triplets had no time for anyone else. At least not until they'd been all over him, demanded the attention they needed, and then with their peanut-sized attention spans, were off to play again.

The difference had seemed like a moment of rest. Or, rather, a nanosecond of one. And one he wasn't altogether sure he was ready for. His boys were his life. Yeah, they were going to grow up, grow away—even if, as he hoped, they stuck around and ranched with him—but at two?

Still, he had to take them back for one more day. Or half day. Just until after noon. He'd do naptime.

Or so he thought.

A springing heifer in distress held Noah up from the

after-lunch pickup time on Tuesday, and the boys had seemed to enjoy their mat story time. Charlie had. It had been about a goggie. Noah translated to "doggy." And as Charlie told him the story in his own vernacular, Henry seemed to understand and agree with claps, nods and his own attempts at words.

Sounds that Noah couldn't yet decipher into English.

Gavin stomped his feet at the telling. Slowly. One at a time. Engaging. Which made Noah smile with gratitude.

And to decide that maybe Little Cowpokes had been a good idea after all.

Each morning Lucy was there to greet his little men, and all three of them, even Gavin, trotted eagerly through the door to the playrooms with her. By day three, none of them looked back at him as they headed off for fun.

And every afternoon, Lucy was the one who brought his crew out to him. *MeWoo* Charlie continued to call her.

"Miss Lucy. *Me*, for Miss, and *Woo* is what he took from Lucy," the young woman had told him with a smile as he finally made it in for pickup just after three on the next Tuesday afternoon. "I'm guessing *l*'s are hard for this age. He's got the *ee* down pat!" Her grin had grown, until she'd met his gaze head-on.

After that, he couldn't say. He'd looked away. The woman was ten years his junior. As a single father with a ranch to run and triplets to raise, he had his hands overfull.

And he was spending far too much time basking in the relief of having a woman respond so enthusiastically, with so much energy, to his crew. Exactly what he'd expected to see from their mother. And had spent months hoping and praying he'd eventually see.

Before she left them all for good.

He was earlier dropping off Wednesday morning. His heifer was looking like she was going to deliver a week early and because she was birthing the first offspring of his recently purchased full-bred Angus bull—a bull he saw as his eventual retirement plan—he had to be present. The boys' futures, their college tuitions could be shaped by the reputation Noah built with his cattle.

Lucy approached as he wheeled the stroller in the door. "Everything okay?" she asked, reaching for Gavin, who was in his arms because he'd been fussy.

"Fine," he rattled off his usual response to the question. One he'd perfected from the time they'd heard they were having triplets. A word he'd repeated multiple times a day during the months before the boys' premature births, and those following as well. Trying to convince Joanna that they would be just fine.

Standing with Gavin on her hip, while her mother helped another client over by the desk, Lucy said, "You don't look fine. Something wrong with the boys?"

Charlie's straps were undone, leaving him to crawl out of the stroller on his own, and Noah was reaching for Henry's safety fastenings, but paused to glance up at the question.

The concern shining from the adult blue eyes focused on him sent a bolt through Noah. Then he realized that Little Cowpokes had a very real stake in the well-being of the children they were caring for.

Turning back to Henry, who was kicking his feet against the bottom of the stroller, Noah said, "Other than a tantrum that soaked the floor during a toy fight during bathtime this morning, the Trent men are doing great," he told her.

Henry free, he turned to see Lucy reaching for Charlie's hand with her free one, while Gavin was pulling at yet another bead in the woman's hair. A unicorn, Noah was pretty sure. Maybe a horse.

Her brow was furrowed, but she neither held Charlie in a death grip, nor made any motion to get her hair out of Gavin's wet fingers, as she said, "What then?"

Noah told her about the heifer. Also a purebred. And part of his hope for the future. Heard himself mention premature bleeding. And stopped abruptly. Definitely not daycare conversation.

"Take all the time you need this afternoon," Lucy said. "I'll stay as late as necessary. And I can find something to feed the boys for dinner if it gets that late."

The sincerity in her offer struck him. Her ease with his children—who were unpredictable and messy at best—hit even deeper. "I can always send my mom or dad in," he told her. "No reason to hold you over." He'd meant to stop there. But smiled instead and added, "I appreciate the offer, though." More than she knew. Or would ever know.

"Seriously," she told him, looking down with a smile as Henry grabbed the bottom of her jean shorts. "I'm not doing anything tonight. And living at home until I find a place of my own..." She shot a glance over toward her mother who was deep in conversation with a woman holding a little one at least a few months younger than Noah's three—and then continued, "I'm happy for the excuse to have someplace to be." The last was issued with a half grimace, half grin, and Noah grinned back.

"Well, thanks," he said, and then headed back out to his SUV, feeling better prepared to face what the day would bring.

As it turned out, the heifer's early delivery posed no issues for either mama or her bull calf. A fact he eagerly shared with Lucy and all three boys when he walked back in for pickup that afternoon. "Baby cooah," Charlie said, clapping his hands. "Me see baby cooah."

Henry clapped, too. Gavin, watching them both, lifted a foot and stomped it down, then repeated with his other foot. A few times.

Lucy's grin was all for Noah that time. "Congratulations," she said, her tone filled with depth. As though she understood the vital importance of the birth to the future.

"So we'll see you tomorrow?" she asked as she walked with him to the door, peeking down into the stroller as she did so, touching each of the three boys there on the tips of their noses.

After days of taking on two-year-old Trent energy, curiosity, shyness and stubbornness, Lucy's continued eagerness to see his miniature men, to spend all day with them, filled Noah's heart in a brand-new way.

Which sent up definite warning signals as he nodded and smiled at the woman who was like a breath of fresh air in a life reeking with responsibility.

And shot him up with a load of guilt, too. So much so that when he took a glance in the nursery just after seven that night, stood there alone in the doorway, watching three little bodies in slumber, checking by rote for breathing movement, he pulled his phone out of his pocket.

He quietly shut the door as he tapped Joanna's name in his contacts list. Maybe she'd want to see the boys. They were older. Had shown some independence.

"Noah?" The woman he'd once considered his best friend picked up on the first ring. "Is everything okay?"

"Fine," he gave her the rote answer. Knowing it was what she needed. Realizing, too, as soon as he heard her voice that nothing had changed. Joanna needed calm... fine...okay, at all costs.

As hard as she'd tried, she'd been unable to find a healthy place for herself in the chaos that children brought to a home. And with them, multiplied by three all at once. The harder she'd tried, only to end up snapping or screaming at the top of her lungs, the worse home life had become. She'd begun to dislike herself. He'd started to resent her inability to mother their boys with the gusto and energy, the desire, that they deserved. And yet, he didn't blame her for not being able to do so. She was who she was. Who she'd always been. He'd been too blinded by his own life plans—understood from birth—to see that she didn't share the vision.

Just as she'd been too focused on the peace and companionship in their home to create friction by speaking up about her own needs for the future. That it contain just the two of them. Alone. Forever.

"I was just thinking about you," he said awkwardly into the silence. He was the one who'd reached out. "Wondering how things are going."

He truly had had a thought along those lines earlier in the day. When the calf had come in perfect health—

the next step in the plan to build a secure future for
their boys.

"Things are actually really good," she said, her tone
more like the girl he'd known in high school than the de-
feated wife and mother she'd become. "I love Colorado.
It's different than Montana, but still…you know, moun-
tains. And this ranch, Noah…the horses… I had no idea
that they were such cognizant creatures. Being part of
training them as therapy animals…it's like… I'm finally
contributing something really worthwhile to the world."

Settling down on the end of his bed, Noah nodded.
Smiled through the sadness. "It's good to hear your
voice," he told her honestly. They hadn't been meant to
be spouses, but they'd been great friends. "You sound
happy."

"I am happy." He heard the truth through the bit of
sorrow her tone had taken on. Happy without the havoc
their children had brought into their world. And then
she asked, "How are the boys?"

"Good!" he told her, standing. Heading downstairs
to the dishes yet to be cleaned. The load of laundry that
had to be moved to the dryer before it mildewed. Telling
her about their first week and a half in daycare.

"I'm glad they're doing well," she said when he fell
silent. There was love in the words. And a hint of the
distance that had been between her and her babies even
before they were born. It had taken him a while to understand Joanna's anxiety around the boys, but she'd done
the right thing, giving him full custody. Giving them the
right to a life without her constant tension.

Words came out of him even as he knew they
shouldn't. "You want to see them?" he asked. "I've got

a new foal that I'm looking to sell. I could donate it to your program there. Use it as a tax write-off..."

He gave himself a mental bop on the head as his words trailed off. And was almost relieved when she said, "I can't right now, Noah. I was going to call and let you know... I've actually started college. Taking summer classes, just to get caught up on some basics. Then in the fall, I start on a degree in counseling."

A genuine grin split Noah's face as he sat at the kitchen table with three booster seats needing to be cleaned, up against wood that hadn't fared any better. "You found you," he said softly. Something they'd talked about during their non-rancorous divorce.

"Yeah." Her tone had softened. "But...you could send me some videos..."

Noah wasn't sure if she'd asked because a part of her needed the connection with the children she'd birthed, or to comfort him, but he agreed to her request and shot off a few of his most recently recorded snippets from his phone's library as soon as they hung up.

And smiled at the heart emojis she sent back a few minutes later.

He wasn't sorry he'd called her.

The conversation just hadn't helped him get the step back he'd been seeking where Lucy Bernard was concerned.

If anything, speaking with Joanna had him thinking about Lucy more. Comparing the two women.

Unable to deny that the way Lucy treated his boys, the way she gravitated to them, related to them, genuinely seemed to enjoy them, were all things they deserved.

And something their own mother wasn't able to provide for them.

Which meant one thing.

Daycare was no longer optional.

Chapter Three

She hadn't gone to the Tenacity Social Club even once since she'd met the Trent men. Nor had she done anything that could even remotely be considered an attempt to find a non-Noah Trent man to date.

No, Lucy had spent Wednesday night making beads. Out of molding clay. She'd carefully rolled the clay, cut the shapes, carefully inserted a metal pick down the middle to make a hole without disturbing the outer shape, baked them, and then had painted and glossed them.

The rolling, cutting, insertion and baking part had taken a couple of hours. Her parents had been out for the evening, hadn't been home to witness her impromptu, perhaps over-the-top art project. She'd meticulously painted and glossed upstairs in her room.

And Thursday morning, in spite of her mother's attempts to keep her occupied in the back, Lucy was out front, conceivably to get some paper clips, when Noah came in with his boys. Charlie and Henry in the stroller, Gavin in his arms.

The littlest Trent must have been having a rough morning. Not only was his father carrying him, but he had tear streaks on his face.

"What's wrong, little one?" she asked, all thoughts of anything but comforting the sweet child escaping as she moved forward and gently rubbed Gavin's back. Then touched the hair on the back of the little boy's head. Something she'd noticed was a comfort to him when she'd been coaxing him to join in a game of follow the leader a couple of days before.

"Oud!" Charlie exclaimed. Lucy had a glimpse of the boss of the pack throwing himself back and forth against the chest straps holding him in place.

"Uhmmm!" Henry said, following his brother's lead with back-and-forth motions.

Gavin turned to look at them. And then noticed Lucy's hair right by him. Reaching out, he touched the newly fashioned bead there. And reached with his other hand to grab a second one. Sharing a quick glance with Noah—whose expression she couldn't read, but could feel—she reached for the boy.

"You like those?" she asked. Gavin's big blue eyes rose to her face, while his fingers continued to clutch her thin, long, beaded braid.

"Me see!" Charlie said. "Me see! Me see!" With Henry chiming in, "Eee, Eee, Eee!"

The door opened behind Noah, and he scooted the stroller over to allow the newcomers entry.

"Hey, Lila," he said, while bending to Charlie's straps. "How's Hank?"

"Doin' fine," the woman in her thirties called as Angela came from the back to greet the newcomer and her eight-month-old baby boy, Hank Jr.

Lucy heard Lila mention something about being late for a dentist appointment as she rushed back out the door, just as Charlie climbed out of his stroller. And taking Gavin with her, she cut the little guy off before he could get near the entrance, while Noah worked on Henry's straps.

"Me see! Me see!" Charlie's voice grew louder with his second demand immediately on top of the first, his fingers opening and closing as he reached both arms up toward the beads in his brother's hands.

Grinning, her heart flooding with the results of her hours of effort the night before, Lucy bent down and pulled one of the two thin braids over her shoulder, letting Charlie get his hands on the beads. Noah lifted Henry out of the stroller and put him down. The third Trent toddler practically tripped over his own legs as he made a beeline for Charlie, at Lucy's back.

"Cooah!" Charlie said. "Cooah say moo!"

"Ooo. Ooo." Henry's voice chimed in happily, while Gavin continued to look between the beads in his hands and Lucy's face.

"Okay, guys, let Miss Lucy stand up." Noah's voice held a note of humor, but both Charlie and Henry let go of the beads in her hair and stepped back.

Gavin continued to sit contentedly on her hip as she rose to find Noah eyeing the beads almost as closely as his sons had. "Cow beads? Where on earth did you find them?"

Chin up, she looked straight at him and said, "I made them." Daring him to make something of that.

"You made them." Noah's words brought her gaze back to him.

She shrugged. "I make lots of things."

"When did you make them?"

He liked her beads. Or liked that she'd worn them. His tone was…saying so.

"Last night."

Gavin lifted her braid and tried to stick a bead between her lips. She grinned, lowered the bead and kissed the boy's forehead.

Then glanced back at his father, who'd watched the exchange. His gaze grew curiously serious for a second, and then lightened as he said, "You trying to bribe my boys with beads?"

"And if I am?" She couldn't keep the challenge out of her voice. Didn't even want to try.

"Lucy? Did you find the paper clips?" Angela's voice interrupted, kindly, but clearly, too.

Right. Lucy's reason for being out front. To get the over-sized thick plastic paperclips they needed to hang colored swatches on a string for one of the day's activities. Her pathetic excuse to see the single older man with triplet two-year-olds.

"I did," she said, bending down to pick them up from the ledge where she'd put them to pick up Gavin. "Here they are." She handed them to Angela, who, after thanking her, remained behind the counter.

"I'll see you this afternoon," Noah nodded, and, after a fist bump with all three boys, starting with Gavin, pushed his empty stroller out the door.

Lucy reached for Henry's hand, said, "Come on, Charlie," and pushed a shoulder against the door leading to the playrooms.

Looking forward to the day.

And to afternoon pickup, too.

But the smile on her face dimmed a little when Angela approached her after she'd settled Gavin down for naptime, nodding toward her to come out to the hallway, and then said softly, "You need to be careful, Lucy," she said. "It's not a good idea to get involved with clients."

The older woman nodded through the window toward the two-year-olds on their mats, eyes closed as they listened to the story Elaina was reading to them while relaxation music played softly in the background.

"I'm not getting involved," Lucy assured her temporary boss, irritated, and yet, knowing that Angela's observation was fair. Appropriate.

And also influenced by Elaina, her close friend, partner and Lucy's overprotective mother.

Reminding herself that she was only at the daycare as a temporary fill-in until she found a remote job in her field, Lucy turned to head out front—her naptime duty—but didn't miss Angela's softly uttered, "Not yet," as she pushed through the door.

Noah kept an eye on the clock Friday afternoon, pickup on his mind. He'd had a good week. One of the best in a long while. Had been able to get more work done in five days than he'd managed to accomplish in almost a month.

Because his mind hadn't been filled with constant concern about the boys. Imagining ways they were getting into trouble while his parents did their best to continue on with their lives and responsibilities while also taking on Noah's. Nor had he been at all worried about them at daycare.

He hadn't had to break for an hour for lunch that sometimes stretched into two because Charlie didn't like to go down for a nap and if the other two missed, they were all miserable.

Mostly, he hadn't had to worry that his little men weren't getting all of the stimulation their young minds needed. Or that they'd hurt themselves on some normal household time, like the corner of the coffee table.

They were in a safe, completely toddler-proof environment.

And he'd missed them like hell. Was looking forward to an evening off to let them rule the roost. No plans other than that they all had to eat. Just him and his boys. In the barn, if they wanted to see the heifer calf. Or the living room if they wanted some instructional television time.

For sure, they'd end the night in his king-size bed, falling asleep to some children's show. After which he'd carefully carry them, one at a time, to their own toddler beds.

It was all planned right down to the part where all four of the Trent men would have to spend the next couple of days without seeing Miss Lucy's smiling face.

Unless…he stepped into Little Cowpokes without allowing himself to complete the thought.

A mistake as it turned out, because the damned thing completed itself once he saw her with his sons in the reception area.

As she helped him strap the boys in their stroller, he asked, "You have plans for the weekend?" Noah's question had been gaining desperation for release as the minutes available for its appearance slipped quickly by.

"Other than watching the wind blow, you mean?" Lucy chuckled. Very much a nonanswer. Clearly the woman kept herself busy. Those beads she'd made hadn't been an amateur attempt.

But he took encouragement from the plans she'd hadn't attached herself to, figuring that she'd left herself open to possibility, and said, "I could use a babysitter."

As soon as the words came out he felt himself grow hot. Hearing the mistake. Treating her like she was some kind of high school kid. Because he, with his failed marriage and three kids, felt so much older than she was.

"If you're offering me the job, I'm happy to accept," Lucy's words came with the click of Gavin's strap and she stood, to look over the top of the filled stroller, straight at him. Her gaze was steady, but not filled with her usual fun as she asked, "You got a date?"

"Hell no." He stopped. Said, "Heck no," and then shrugged. "I've got some fencing work to do—a two-man job—and Ryder—my brother—who lives in the big house with Mom and Dad, but has his own ranch duties, is free to help. Mom and Dad generally watch the boys when I'm busy with work that involves power tools and big animals roaming in fields, but Dad has someone coming to look at some horses. My sister Renee had offered to help Mom—she and her fiancé live in a blue bungalow on the property, very chic, but there's some big sale going on in Bronco and she and my little sister, Cassie who lives at home and also helps with the boys, want to go look at wedding dresses. Renee just got engaged."

"Right, to Miles Parker," Lucy said. Just that, nothing more. Giving him no indication of what she did and did not know about his family.

Or him.

"So, you up for hanging out with my mom and help-ing out?" he asked. Then, hearing how he was asking a beautiful young woman to spend her weekend off, he said, "I'll pay you double whatever babysitters get these days," and without a breath added, "More an hour than you make here." The offer came with him having no idea how much she made at Little Cowpokes.

Rolling his eyes, he stopped. Looking for some way to joke his way out of having even asked any questions at all. Taking back any need for her assistance.

Before he got there, Lucy's smile returned and she said, "Are you kidding me? A chance to spend time with these three handsome dudes without other kiddos need-ing my attention as well? You're on." She glanced down into the stroller as she spoke, and then back up at him.

Staring her down, Noah wanted to know if she found him handsome as well. But thankfully was able to keep that last wondering silent.

And got himself and his brood out of there before any of them could do something to make her change her mind.

She was just babysitting. As Lucy insisted to her mother multiple times on Saturday when she announced that she'd be out all day and not to plan dinner for her. She'd get something on her own in town.

Maybe visit the Tenacity Social Club. During her years in Bronco, she'd heard the band that was perform-ing in town that night. Had really liked them.

The story appeased her mother enough that Elaina at least kept her warning comments to herself. And told her to say hi to Olive Trent, and to thank her again for the fabric Olive had donated to the Tenacity Quilting Club, in which Elaina was very active.

Her mother had been dealt with. Too bad Lucy's emotional cortex hadn't been as easily appeased. She might not be heading out to a daytime date, but she was as excited as if she was. Inarguably—in her opinion—the most handsome man in town, who also happened to be single, had invited her to his family's ranch. To spend the day with his mother and kids.

When everyone knew she'd long outgrown the post of high school babysitter she'd once held so proudly. Knew, too, that there were always available high school girls in town eager to make money by looking after others' children.

And a family like the Trents—long established and knowing pretty much everyone—would surely have their pick of the best of them.

But Noah had chosen Lucy.

And had sent very definite man-to-woman signals when he'd issued the request to watch his three boys for the day.

Signals that continued to send out vibes the second she pulled underneath the Stargazer arch and saw the big off-road vehicle with three filled car seats on the back-seat bench.

Noah had come to greet her.

The road she was on led to a big barn first, and...beyond that she didn't know. Had never actually been on the property before.

She'd heard a lot about it recently, though, as she assumed everyone else in town had. The money that had been stolen from the town fifteen years before had just been found intact, based, at least partially, on the arch she'd just passed beneath. The stars across the top of the arch had contained three words—Look, Juniper, and Rock—had led Winona Ryder and Stanley Sanchez, the town's oldest newlyweds, to find the missing money that had been buried under rocks at Stooler's ranch all those years.

And…she'd expected to find her way to the big house without a problem. There was only one road that she could see—and a big house was pretty obvious once an even bigger barn was no longer blocking it.

Having Noah there to greet her was a much nicer start to the day. Smiling, she rolled down the window of the little pickup truck, and when he called out to follow him, nodded. Then waved at the boys before rolling up her window.

He'd come to get her.

You didn't do that unless you were trying to make someone really feel welcome. Right? Or, at least, wanting to make a good first impression.

He was a little late on that score. Been there. Done that. The previous week.

In jeans, a purple T-shirt with colorful hearts all over it, and tennis shoes that matched, Lucy parked where Noah pointed as they reached his parents' home, and opened her door, hearing "MeWoo!" and then "Woo! Woo!" before her feet had even touched the ground.

"Good morning!" she said to the group as a whole, joining Noah at the four-wheeler to unstrap Gavin while he worked on the other two.

It wasn't that she preferred Gavin to Charlie and Henry. With those three, there was no choosing. Each of them had already claimed equal pieces of her heart—separate and apart from their father's impact on her. But Gavin was… Gavin. Though she wasn't even sure what that meant. He just seemed, not needier, but…shier, absolutely…and also…more in need of hugs.

As soon as Charlie and Henry were free they rushed up to the steps leading to the back door of the house and disappeared inside. Olive and Christopher Trent stood smiling in the doorway. Calling out a warm welcome.

That was when Lucy knew that she was more than just one in a line of babysitters. What more, or how much of it, remained to be seen.

Chapter Four

Noah wasn't in the house two minutes before he felt superfluous. With their grandparents *and* MeWoo both at their beck and call, his boys were in their elements. In a home they'd known since birth, with their familiar toys to get into, and three adults doting on them, the two olders barely gave him a hug as he left.

Gavin, sitting contentedly on Lucy's hip, waved with the hand not holding the horse beads in the day's thin braids amid her wavy blond hair.

The sight made him a bit gooey inside and he high-tailed it out without looking back. Turned his thoughts to the newest babies in his world—the Angus kind. Nearing the end of his calving season, Noah had an emergency repair that couldn't wait. A section of fencing surrounding the new mamas and their heifer and bull calves had been downed by a spruce tree hit by lightning. Not something many Montana farmers would have to deal with during calving, since the most common time to calve was winter months.

But Noah had been given the go-ahead to start his own cattle business while still in high school, and while he'd missed a lot of school for the ranch in general, he couldn't be up nights, or checking calves every two hours for six weeks straight. So he'd set his calving schedule for May and June. By the time he'd graduated, he'd been in full swing and hadn't been about to interrupt the success.

In the two years since the triplets were born, he'd had to hire hands to do the night shifts while his cows were birthing their offspring. But the rest was still pretty much on him.

And he wouldn't have it any other way.

The one thing he'd gotten absolutely right in his life was knowing that his place was on the Stargazer. He'd been born there. Figured he'd die there old and gray, too. It was the life he'd been born to. The only life that felt right to him.

As he grabbed the supplies he'd need, loading them into the back of his truck, Noah's thoughts came to an abrupt halt. His life...the ranch...had all suited Joanna. And he'd been so single-focused he'd just assumed she'd seen that having offspring to work the ranch with him as he got older, offspring to carry on the ranch when he was gone, was as much a necessary part of their lives as the land and cattle that supported them.

He'd been so intent on the life he'd been born to, he hadn't considered that hers had been on a separate path.

That the vision she'd formed growing up had been a complete antithesis to his.

He'd texted Ryder, who was already out on the ranch on horseback, to let his brother know he was heading out. Horse and man were already at the site, clearing away tree branches by the time Noah arrived.

With a nod at Ryder across the expanse of branches,

Noah went right to work. Eager to use his hands, to expend the odd new note of energy that had been flowing through him all week, as he adjusted to a new normal where his boys were finding their first real tastes of independence from him. There were some pangs of loss over what had been that would never be again—midnight cuddles with a wrapped bundle suckling at the bottle he held. Knowing he was the whole world to three incredible human beings. Winter Sunday afternoons lying on a quilt on the carpet of his living room—he and his little guys who weren't yet crawling, with wood and flames sparking in the fireplace several feet away, and sports on the television.

There was also a load of relief. Knowing that his boys had bonded with Lucy—and it seemed like she with them—and that they were not only safe, but secure and happy in his absence, was…nice.

Lucy. He'd watched her introduce herself to his parents, wearing a smile as she carried his son into Noah's childhood home, at ease as though she'd been there many times before.

And he'd bugged out.

Because part of him had wanted to stay. To be a part of the interaction.

Or…just to watch it go down.

"What?" Ryder's somewhat irritated question pulled Noah from his thoughts. Heaving the branch he'd just broken off to the pile of them growing in his truck, Noah looked over at another Trent guy he loved. And had fought with more times than he could count, too.

"What, what?" he asked, gloved hands at his sides

instead of reaching for the saw that was going to cut the thick trunk down to movable sizes.

"You were shaking your head. You don't want me sawing this end?"

Of course he did. No way he'd get the work done alone in one day. "Yeah, saw, that's fine," he said, reaching for his own chainsaw, his hand on the pull lever to get it going.

He didn't get the chance. Ryder was heading straight for him. "What?" Noah asked that time. The saw didn't start? Ryder hadn't checked his fuel level? "There's a couple of cans of motor mix in the front of the bed," he said, nodding toward the truck.

Then, glancing at Ryder's horse, added, "And treats behind my seat."

His brother went for the water that was always in a cooler on the floor of the passenger side of Noah's truck. Helped himself to a bottle, uncapped the lid and took the whole thing down in nonstop swallows.

Re-capping the empty bottle, Ryder tossed the container into the truck bed and said, "You haven't said a word since you got here," then, after that brilliant pronouncement added, "What's got you so distracted?"

"Who says I'm distracted?" Noah grouched, pulling on the cord of the chainsaw. Making quick work of the half of the trunk on his side of the fencing. And stood to see Ryder still standing where he'd left him. Eating an apple instead of drinking water.

Watching him. Not sawing his half of the heavy trunk.

"It's Lucy Bernard," Ryder said, a knowing smirk

on his face. "Mom said she was coming to help out at the house today."

Bending, Noah grabbed the heaviest piece of trunk, slinging it up to balance on his shoulder and headed toward the truck. "I'm a single father," he said as he passed his brother. "I found a babysitter. Comes with the job."

If he kept himself busy enough, he might have moments where he could believe himself on that one. Claiming that all he'd done was find a babysitter.

He had to believe it, of course. No option there. Not only was Lucy ten years younger than him, but he had no room in his life to take on anything else. Not even thoughts of going out with the captivating woman. And even if he did, there was no way in hell he'd ask someone just starting out with her life to saddle herself with three lively as yet untutored men along with their father.

And that was the only way he presented.

He tossed his log as though it weighed little more than a football. Felt some satisfaction at the loud clunk it made against the inside of the truck.

"Ha!" Ryder said, sending his apple core a good baseball's throw into the pasture. "Lucy's on the top list of Tenacity hotties. Even you'd have to notice," the younger man continued.

Noah seriously considered why he'd accepted his brother's offer to help with the fence repair. Breathing back a surge of anger, he picked up another log, settled it on his shoulder and stepped right in front of Ryder.

Pushing his nose up in his little brother's face he said, "You stay away from her, you hear me?" he said, clear warning apparent in his tone. "She's not your type."

Noah wasn't sure any woman was Ryder's type. The

playboy's roving eye didn't bode well for anyone who might develop real feelings for him.

"Ha!" Ryder said again, but showed the good sense of taking a step back as he did so. "You're jealous!"

Noah tossed his log. Hard. "I am not jealous," he asserted.

Ignoring the fact that he was kind of afraid he could be.

"And it wouldn't matter if I was," he added, because one thing Noah always had to be honest. Most particularly since he'd taken on the burden of a failed marriage. "I'm no catch," he said, hauling up two slightly smaller logs, one on each shoulder. "I'm divorced, work seven days a week, have three kids entering their terrible twos all at once, and two ranch mutts that I let stay in the house at night."

He'd done the math. More than once in the two weeks since he'd met Lucy Bernard.

He dumped his logs, Ryder's sudden silence hanging like a death sentence over his head, and on his way back to grab the last two logs said, "And to tell you the truth, bro, after all that's happened, I'm not even sure I'd want to be caught."

Truth.

One that left a door open that he couldn't seem to make himself slam shut.

Lucy was having way too much fun. On the floor, focusing just on the triplets, she was learning so much more about their individualities. Gavin liked to hold things in his hand. Seemed to have more courage, more gumption, when he had something in at least one hand.

Give him something to hold and he'd try a taste of something new to eat, rather than just stand there and shake his head. Charlie didn't boss the others around so much as they followed him. The oldest triplet took it in stride, though. He was the best of the three at sharing. And Henry...he was quite content to wander off into his own world and amuse himself there. While keeping an eye on his brothers, of course. He, like a lot of people, exhibited the old FOMO. Fear of missing out.

A term Lucy had heard in marketing strategy meetings too many times. And part of the reason she'd left the lucrative job she'd had and done well at. Her idea of spreading the word was to highlight good in a product or idea. Not finding ways to manipulate peoples' minds so they'd spend their hard-earned money on things they didn't really need or want. Things they wouldn't ordinarily buy and might end up not using.

Growing up in Tenacity had taught her how precious every dollar could be to household budgets. And to the people who worked long hours to earn just enough to make it, with very little to spare.

With all three boys lined up in tiny, fur-covered foam armchairs that fit them perfectly, with a toddler-appropriate educational show on the flat-screen TV mounted on the wall opposite them, Lucy wandered out to the kitchen where Olive was preparing lunch for them.

And for the adult male Trents, too, who'd be coming to the main house for lunch about an hour after the littles ate.

"Can I help?" she asked, used to being her mother's sidekick during meal preparation. With the three boys being so full of energy all morning, she and Olive had managed a sentence or two of adult conversation, but mostly to tag-team the triplets.

"You've been more help than you can imagine," the woman said kindly, smiling. "I've got this. Had everything prepared before breakfast this morning. You keeping an eye on the boys for me so I don't worry that one of them is trying to chew on a remote or stick the hand of a doll up his nose, I'll be indebted to you." The young grandmother laughed as she said the words.

Leaving a sense of Olive's bone-deep happiness with her life washing over Lucy.

And Lucy knew, then and there, had complete confirmation, that while she loved her brand of marketing, and believed she had a valuable service she could offer to middle-class families, she was right to move home, too.

Because she needed what Olive had far more than she cared about how she earned her living. She loved Tenacity. Living in a place where the entire town felt like home. Loved knowing who she was and who she was with. Loved knowing what was expected of her and others. She wanted what her parents had.

What Olive and Christopher Trent had.

What Angela and Otis Corey had.

Not just days or months or years filled with money earned, goals met and traveling.

She wanted a life.

One that started young and continued on through old age.

A forever home.

A husband. A house full of children that would grow up and continue to be a part of their lives.

She wanted noise and chaos. Laughter and tears.

Quiet moments like the ones she had sitting on the floor next to the boys' chairs, feeling Gavin's fingers as he reached out for and then held on to the horse bead in her hair.

And messy moments, too, with faces wearing remnants of food smushed by chubby little hands into birdlike mouths. Trays smeared with an array of colors and consistencies, reminding her of a Van Gogh painting she'd seen once. The floor around the three lined-up highchairs dotted with a menagerie of particles, too. Mostly the peas that didn't go over as well as the fruit and cut-up hot dogs.

Lucy noticed Olive watching her as Olive took care of the chairs and floor and Lucy wiped up the triplets, one at a time, jabbering to them the whole time, and set them free to pick a story for naptime. Not sure she wanted to be privy to the older woman's thoughts, or even what she might hope they could be, Lucy was nonetheless uplifted when Olive smiled at her.

More than just the kind offering of a stranger. The look in Olive's eyes carried something deeper. And while Lucy wasn't going there, she was glad to have been the recipient, just the same.

But the best part of the morning came when she sat in an armchair to read the boys the three stories they'd picked and both Henry and Gavin climbed up onto her lap, settling back, one cuddled to each side of her, while Charlie—who wasn't a fan of sleeping during the day— stood beside the chair to look at the pictures on the pages as she turned them.

Wishing she could pull out her phone, to record what would likely just be a few seconds in time—considering the attention span of two-year-olds—Lucy let her heart fill to the brim as she started in on the first book.

Whether she ever saw Noah Trent again in her life, or not, she knew that his moments there had shaped the rest of it. With his sons, he'd shown her who she was.

Who she'd always been.

And always would be.

A modern woman whose ultimate purpose was to be a partner in the home. One who would fully flourish with a husband, home and children.

And with them, would find her ultimate happiness.

Ryder challenged Noah to race back to the main house for lunch. On horseback he could cut through fields that Noah had to drive around. Noah still figured he could take him, and did so, with only a little bit of effort.

Put forth as much because he was eager to check on his mom and Lucy and the boys as any latent desire to show his little brother that he was still the ruler of their world. In a long-ago boyhood sense.

And because his largest motivation had been to witness the dynamic in the house—with the only out of the ordinary change being Lucy Bernard—he stood outside instead, waiting for Ryder to show up.

Ostensibly so he could gloat. Which he did.

And was still doing as he walked first into the house that was still home to Ryder.

His ears picked up the silence first. Something he'd grown used to looking for when he came in for lunch. It meant his tribe had gone down successfully for naps.

His gaze shot to the table. Four place settings. His dad's cowboy hat already hung from his chair—meaning the man was home, ready to eat, and in the bathroom washing up. His mother's place, at the opposite end of the table was set, as were two for him and Ryder.

His heart sank. He hadn't walked around the side of the house to see if Lucy's car was still there. He'd assumed it was.

"When did Lucy go?" he asked.

Frowning, Olive asked, "Go where?"

Noah nodded toward the table. "There's no place set for her." He hadn't paid her yet. Had thought she'd stay the day, not just until naptime.

"She munched a little with the boys and is kind of busy right now. Said she'd eat in a bit." His mother's gaze held a message she didn't speak. Noah wasn't sure he could decipher it, either. Was pretty sure he didn't want to try.

But he moved in the direction of her head nod, as though the woman who'd given him birth still had the ultimate power in directing his course. She didn't. He'd long since moved on from his mother's apron strings.

He was heading toward the living room for one reason alone.

He wanted to see the woman he'd told himself—and his brother—hadn't been distracting him on and off all morning.

Not slowing down his work. But possibly his conversation.

He stopped before reaching his destination. Stood there, looking into the large room where he'd spent every Christmas morning of his life, mesmerized. And listening.

"A sleepy boy sleeps…" Lucy's tone was soft. Pitched

higher. Full of life. And comfort, too, as she sat in his father's chair, reading to his sons.

Two of whom were asleep on her lap, their heads on either side of her neck, resting just above her breasts. And Charlie...whose back was to Noah, lay between her legs, the side of his head on her stomach, facing toward the book.

Noah swallowed.

Blinked.

And his world shifted on its axis.

Chapter Five

Lucy went to church with her parents on Sunday, mostly because they expected her to do so, but excused herself from lunch out with them and a couple of their close friends and headed back to the house. She had laundry to finish. Some cleaning that was overdue.

And, most important, a packet to fill out for a marketing firm in Denver—a prerequisite to the second interview she'd earned for herself. Like the first, it would be virtual.

But instead of just talking to the personnel manager, she'd be meeting with the executives with whom she'd be working.

Out of all the jobs she'd applied for, the Denver job was her top pick by far. Not only was the firm hugely successful, they were known for homing in on their clients' products, making each job personal, not just excelling at getting people to buy things. The company had been around forty years, had impressive yearly earnings, giving her potential opportunity to spend her entire career with them.

The position being offered was remote.

Other than a few weeks for training, she could work from home.

And the signing bonus, along with what she'd saved while working in Bronco, would be enough for her to get a small place of her own.

She already had her eye on a little house that was for sale on a nice, quiet street in town. Not far from the elementary school. It was only two bedrooms, but there was room to expand. She could afford it. And, best of all, it was vacant, so she could move in right away.

Living back home with her parents, while sweet in some ways, was driving her up the wall, too. She was twenty-four, not fourteen.

A fact that Elaina was having a hard time recognizing. Her dad, bless him, was a quiet support for both of them. Which meant he didn't get involved between them.

Lucy had glanced over the Denver pre-interview packet when it had come in through email on Thursday, but had had no real idea how thorough it was. A couple of hours of work, at least.

That turned into three due to the number of times her mind was wandering to Noah and the boys. Were they out on the ranch? At home?

At the main house?

In town? Maybe someplace she could run into them?

In the end, she put on headphones, chose a playlist of her favorite country songs of all time, and forced herself to concentrate on the task at hand.

A job well done, she decided early Monday morning as she gave the packet a last fresh glance and hit Send. And then braided her hair with the new dog beads she'd made the night before.

Charlie and Henry both had their words for cow and horse. Dog was next.

Along with convincing Gavin to find his own words.

She couldn't believe how happy she was to see Noah and his boys show up at the daycare an hour later, and while she admonished herself with a firm warning not to get too attached, she almost picked up the phone and called the single father midmorning, when Gavin gave her a grunt that she took to be the word *dog*. He made the same sound every time she pointed to the bead. It had to mean something.

She'd been about to elicit Noah's confirmation on the matter that afternoon as they stood alone in the reception area of Little Cowpokes. But her thoughts were completely cut off when he stood after buckling in his third son and said, "Thanks again for Saturday. All day yesterday Charlie was saying, 'See MeWoo.' And Henry would nod."

He glanced away as he said the last bit, as though he'd embarrassed himself. Or had said more than he'd wanted to.

Figuring that he didn't want her to read more into what he was saying than was there, she smiled and told him, "I thought of them a lot yesterday, as well." Them. Not him. "They're not only adorable, but a fun challenge, too, distinguishing their different personalities, and making certain that no one gets left behind."

A kicking noise came from the stroller. Gavin. Lifting his foot and dropping it on the floor. Then lifting the other. She didn't have to look over to know. She could tell by the sound. But she couldn't look anyway. She was too busy being engrossed by the blue of Noah's eyes, as he looked at her.

"I'd like to thank you," he said then. "I was thinking, since you missed lunch on Saturday, a dinner out. At Castillo's. Without the tribe. So you can just relax."

Castillo's. Small. Cozy. A little dark. Lucy's heart leaped at the thought of sitting there, across from the hunky cowboy. And so she said, "You paid me far more generously than you should have. You definitely don't owe me any more."

She couldn't go. Not just to pay a debt. She wanted far more than that. Which wasn't at all fair to the man who already had his hands so full, with his spread, the new cows, and handling his boys on his own. Noah had no social life.

Or so she'd been told by Ryder, outside the main house on Saturday, while Noah had been having a last-minute conversation with his mother in the doorway.

Noah had appeared before she'd been able to discern if Ryder had been warning her off, or just warning her in general. Had the younger Trent seen the way Lucy had been trying so hard *not* to look at Noah in front of his family?

"So how about if I just want to take you to dinner? If it's not frowned upon because of some kind of work ethic fraternization."

The question hit her head-on, leaving her with no cautions in place as she practically blurted, "In that case, I accept." And then found enough cognizance to say, "It probably wouldn't be cool here, except that I'm not a regular full-time employee. I'm only helping out my mom while I look for a job."

How his face could seem to light up with pleasure with him not even cracking a smile, Lucy didn't know, but she saw it happen. And gave him a huge grin.

"So… Thursday night okay with you?" he asked, rolling the stroller back and forth as the troops started to get restless inside. "Renee and Miles have been offering to sit with the boys so I can get out now and then. You know how it is with new love…they figure everyone else has to find it too—"

He cut off midsentence. Glanced into the stroller and said, "Just a sec, guys," as though the little ones would just nod and sit back patiently.

Afraid that, after his obvious gaffe, he was going to renege on his offer when his attention returned to her, Lucy said, "Thursday night would be great."

"Seven?" he asked then, a hand reaching into the stroller. "I can feed the boys dinner and get them ready for bed, so Renee and Miles can have half an hour of playtime and then put them down for the night." He turned to face her for the last few words.

Lucy smiled again, just too happy to contain herself, and said, "Seven it is. You want to just meet there?" Her mother would hear about the dinner, of course. But it would seem more like just a friends thing if they drove separately.

"I'll pick you up," Noah said, making her heart soar some more, until he said, "That way if I'm late, you're not holding up a table waiting for me. With these men, you just never know…" His words trailed off.

And while Lucy came down to earth some, realizing that there was a strong possibility Noah really was just being nice, a friend thing, she was still kind of pinching herself an hour after he'd left.

Even with the prospect of having to deal with her mother's hovering, and warnings, on Thursday, Lucy knew for certain that moving home to Tenacity had most definitely been the right choice.

Noah almost scrapped the date. In black jeans instead of his usual blue, with a red-and-black checked shirt and his black dress cowboy boots, he stared in his bathroom mirror and wondered what in the hell he was doing.

He hadn't dressed up for a date since senior prom. With Joanna. Hadn't been on a date with anyone else since then, either.

And yet…there he was going out with someone who'd been in second or third grade when he'd gone to prom. And he was going to show up at the front door of her parents' home—her home—to pick her up. Just as he'd picked up his date in high school.

No.

He shook his head. Pulled out his cell to phone Renee and tell her he was staying home. Then he saw Lucy's new contact listing. And shoved the device back in his pocket. The night wasn't just about him. He'd made an offer, which had been accepted by a woman who did not deserve to be stood up.

Didn't stop him from being besieged by thoughts of what her parents had to be thinking about their only child going out with a divorced man who was ten years her senior and had three kids. Such recriminations pretty much dogged him as he drove into town.

He hadn't told his own parents about the dinner, either. Renee might have. He wasn't open to conversation on the matter, so wasn't asking.

And during those moments when he was past the self-flagellation, he was rather looking forward to the evening. Had felt the anticipation hanging just out of reach all week long. A sensation he hadn't known since his sons had been born.

And life as he'd always known it, and had expected it to be forever, had crashed and burned.

Oddly, any consideration concerning what anyone else thought fled from his mind as he pulled into the drive of the Bernard home and saw Lucy come out the front door, closing it firmly behind her. He might have been thankful for the no-parent participation if he hadn't been so consumed by the short denim skirt that fit perfectly shaped hips, short-sleeved black blouse that hugged her waist and flared enough to grab the top of her hips, and the blond hair—without beads—curled and flowing around her.

And the smile.

Oh, Lord, that smile. He'd been sleeping with it for two weeks. Telling himself over and over that Lucy's ability to accept what came at her with a hint of humor was something he'd exaggerated. Only to think, every time he saw her, that he hadn't.

Jumping out of the truck as she came toward the drive, he started to round his truck, to open her door for her, and then stopped. Was that too high school?

Deciding it would be more awkward just to stand there, or slink back to slide in his seat, he proceeded to open the door. And was glad he had as Lucy's petite size, short skirt and high heels made it a little difficult for her to manage the running board and get up into the seat of his big F-250.

Tempted to just take her hips into his hands and lift her, he held out one hand instead, and braced her weight as she climbed in, saying, "Thank you, sir." Her tone was teasing. Maybe even a bit sexy.

But he heard the *sir*.

And felt old.

Noah wasn't smiling at her. He clearly had something on his mind, but wasn't sharing it. She told herself to simply enjoy the night. The two of them together in his truck...secluded...alone for the first time. He'd dressed up and, oohhh, he did it well. The thighs, shoulders, broad chest... He was the best-looking guy she'd ever gone out with. The awareness just kept hitting Lucy. Freezing her in time and space.

Until she blurted, "Did the boys cry when you left?" Her voice sounded to her like lead dropping in a box.

He was looking in his side mirror as he signaled a turn. "Nope." That was it. Nothing more.

Okay, then. Another turn and they'd be there, she told herself. Maybe they should have brought the boys along for dinner.

Except that she'd spent the past two days running all kinds of delicious scenarios in her mind regarding how the evening would go. Assuming, of course, that they were on a date.

"You cool enough?" Noah asked, reaching for the air-conditioning console.

"Fine."

As thank-you dinners went, the current one was at

suck level. And yet, no way did she want to bail. She just had to figure out how to make Noah smile.

Unless, of course, he was regretting the offer he'd made her.

With that possibility looming a bit too large for her, Lucy still felt a little sedate as she and Noah walked into the restaurant and were led to the booth furthest from the door. Back by the bar. Most out of the way. Which meant they had to walk by pretty much everyone else seated there. She nodded at a parent from the daycare. He nodded at...well, pretty much everyone.

And suddenly, she was glowing. Feeling more beautiful than she'd ever felt in Tenacity. A woman in the hall of fame. And so excited to be there. She felt lucky. Wealthy. Happy. And hoping that what some of the people were most likely wondering—whether she and Noah were lovers—became a definite yes.

Right up until they sat down, him facing the room, her back to it, and he went immediately for the menu.

Hiding behind it?

With others surreptitiously looking on? Not that all that much was discernible in the intimate lighting.

But really, what would everyone think of him using the menu as a wall between them? Like he didn't already know it by heart? Along with everyone else in town?

It wasn't like there were pages of unexpected options. Or even one new item.

"Hey, Noah, haven't seen you in here in forever," Yolanda Castillo stood there—in her early sixties, the friendly woman looked exactly the same to Lucy as she had when Lucy had been a four-year-old coming in with her parents for a plain bean-and-cheese burrito. "And,

Lucy, good to see you back in town. Your mom tells me you're planning to stay?"

"I am," she said, smiling. Far too aware that Noah hadn't said anything yet. He'd lowered the menu, though. She took that as a win.

Yolanda's smile appeared exactly as it always did as she looked between the two of them and asked, "Can I get you something from the bar?" As if Lucy and Noah were regulars.

Or had been seen together before. Ever.

"I'd like a beer," Noah said, turning his electric blue eyes on the restaurant's owner of more than thirty years. Half owner. Yolanda's husband, Pablo, the chef, was the other half. With their older son tending...

Lucy's thought broke off as Noah's gaze turned toward her. "How about you? Beer? Wine? Something stronger?"

What, he thought she was going to need a strong libation to get through dinner? Lucy looked at Yolanda and said, "Can I have a peach margarita, please?" She wasn't driving.

More like celebrating. She was on a date—maybe— with Noah Trent! Even if she wasn't—she had him to herself for an entire meal.

Since they were sitting right by the bar, Yolanda only had a few steps to go to place their order. She chatted with her older son, the bartender, as he made Lucy's margarita. She knew because she was watching them.

While Noah looked at the menu some more.

Waiting on his beer to take the edge off being with someone he barely knew? He was definitely sending out second-thought vibes.

The couple of minutes it took for the drinks to get there seemed like an hour. Yolanda set them down with a quick "I'll be right back to get your order," before rushing off to a table up front.

Lucy glanced at Noah. To see him picking up his beer and looking straight at her. "Cheers," he said, his mug hanging there between them. Picking up her salt-rimmed glass, she clunked his mug—trying so hard not to get her salt in his beer, that she spilled a bit of her tequila-based libation on the table.

Great. Shoot me now. Lucy thought, taking a larger sip than she'd normally have done. And liking the sting and then warmth as it went down, took another. For liquid courage.

She wasn't driving.

And might need to be able to forget the night.

Setting her glass down, she wiped at the part she'd wasted, and then glanced up, expecting to see Noah's menu again.

She saw him studying her instead. "What?" she asked, tensing as she waited for his response, fearing that the missive would include something about dinner being a mistake, with an apology attached at the end. Or some such.

"I just...didn't intend for this to be so awkward," he told her. "It's been so long since I've been on a date—seriously. I got married twelve years ago, and was exclusive with Joanna for years before that. Not meant to excuse my lack of aplomb, but at least let you know that it's not you."

The fact that he looked her in the eye through the entire bulletin touched Lucy as much as his words had done. Warmed her. To the point of her being a flooded puddle at his feet.

She'd never been out with a guy who was man enough to show her a vulnerability.

And…he'd just confirmed that they really were on a date!

Leaning forward, she folded her hands and let her gaze devour his as she said, "So, I went on this date once with a marketing executive from another company—we met at a conference in Denver—and anyway, he'd said we were going out for steak, so I'm thinking…steak house, you know. I wore a denim skirt, cowboy boots, a red-checked shirt with some frills that I wore for a rodeo I was in during high school, and a glitzy bolo tie.

"He takes me downtown to valet-park his Jaguar, and then up in a private elevator to this revolving restaurant where everyone, including him, is dressed in like black-tie apparel. Not all black, but you get the idea. Let me tell you, the jewels that glittered in the place were real. Not cheap, glued-on rhinestones like I'd plastered all over my bolo tie…"

His gaze didn't waver. It was like she was the only person in the place, and Lucy just kept right on. "The menu was in French—I'd never heard of a French steak house—but I took it as my second language in college, so managed to hold my own there. Better than I did during our predinner conversation. We both spoke English, but we were definitely talking different languages. I tried to make a joke about my bolo tie, told him that it had blinded a bulldogger in the ring and instead of bringing down the steer, it almost got him. He looked at me like I had mac and cheese smeared all over my face. Not only had he never been to a rodeo, but he didn't know what a bulldogger was. Thought I was talking about some old TV show from before I was born that had a sportscaster named Bulldog…" With a shrug, Lucy felt heat creep up her skin for the second it took her to see the glint of admiration that was shining brighter than the humor in Noah's gaze. "That was the least awkward moment," she said and then shrugged. "He was talking about kinds of boats I'd never heard of, fancy trips he wanted to take, asking me what my biggest dream was, and when I said to become a wife and mother, you'd think that I'd told him I wanted to be a serial killer. That's when I realized, if I had to work so hard to impress the guy, he wasn't the right one."

It had been one of the last dates she'd been on before moving home. She'd learned a lot about herself that night. Or had seen clearly what she'd already known. She needed someone who would accept her warts and all. Someone who understood where she came from, saw the value in family—and putting it first.

"I need to be with someone who understands me. And doesn't judge. We all have flaws." She had no idea why she put that out there so boldly. Almost as a challenge. But she didn't regret having done so.

Noah didn't retreat, or seem at all taken aback by her words.

He leaned in toward her. "How long did you have to sit there with him?" he asked, not smiling anymore, but just as intent on her as he'd been since she'd started her story.

"Not long. I actually developed a stomachache—for real, though not as acute as I pretended—and asked him to call me a cab. I left the guy sitting alone at a table for two in a five-star restaurant, with drinks on the table and food on the way."

She was who she was. And it wasn't always pretty.

She'd never told another soul about that night.

But didn't regret having shared it with Noah.

Opening herself up to him just felt...right.

Chapter Six

Flaws. She needed to be with someone who accepted her flaws and all. Sitting back, listening while Lucy ordered fajitas with no guacamole or green peppers, Noah wasn't sure the woman had any flaws. Knowing what she wanted wasn't a bad thing.

Being able to express those wants was pretty much at the top of his list of things about her that impressed him.

And spoke to him deeply, too.

Joanna hadn't been able to speak up for herself. Not until that self had been so trapped that her speaking up had entailed screaming bouts with accusations and complaints flying all over the place.

Sessions that had always ended up with her in tears, and begging for forgiveness.

Which hadn't sat well with him, either. After she'd taken it all back, he'd never been sure what, exactly, he'd done to upset her, and so had no way of knowing for sure how to not repeat the mistake. Had tried his best to pay attention, read between the lines, look for triggers.

They'd just never seemed to be the same ones.

Not until he'd understood the real problem.

And saw his own culpability in its existence.

Lucy had excused herself to the restroom as soon as they'd ordered, and his mental Joanna segue had him wondering if he'd made Lucy's stomach hurt, too. Like Black Tie had done.

"Sorry," she said, smiling at him as she slid back into her side of their booth. "I have to pee sometimes when I get nervous or excited. That's TMI, too much information. And the margarita isn't helping."

Contrary to too much information, Noah didn't have enough. Which was, nervous or excited?

Reaching a hand across the table, he slid it beneath her fingers and held on. Just fingers touching fingers. "I'm going to hope that tonight's trip was excitement-based," he said, even as he wondered what in the hell he was doing.

He had nothing to offer any woman. Let alone one as young, as vibrant, as at-the-beginning-of-her-entire-future, as Lucy was.

Her lips trembled a bit at the corners, as she smiled. And he said, "Do something for me?"

She blinked. Pulled her hand from his, which—while he'd rather have continued to maintain contact—was a smart move. She reached for her salt-rimmed glass, raised it to her lips and said, "Of course," and then sipped.

"For however long or short we know each other, speak your mind. Without apology. Whether it's to say you want to be a wife and mother, or fly to the moon naked and eat green cheese. Speak it." If she could do that...he could see himself able to be her friend. If nothing else.

She shook her head, grinning. "Of course," she told him. And then her expression straightened, her gaze seeming to be reading him.

Not completely uncomfortable by the idea, he sat there and let her. Kind of curious to see how far off the mark she'd end up.

"So... I guess I have something I have to ask, too," she finally said.

Lifting the bottom of his beer bottle out toward her he said, "Shoot." Took a long sip. Curious, and a little bit eager to hear where she'd ended up.

"The boys' mother..."

That was it. Three words. Not a question at all.

It was as if she'd read his mind. Or known the thought process he'd had while she'd been gone, which had prompted his request of her.

But because she'd hit the bull's-eye, and because, curiously, her having done so didn't bother him, he said, "What about her?"

"What happened?"

Which version of town gossip was true, he translated. Allowing that the question was fair. One he'd have expected if he'd bothered to think about the night from Lucy's perspective.

He opened his mouth, ready to give his rote response—growing apart, lives taking different roads—and, instead, said, "I failed her." The whole truth. In three words.

"How?"

They were on a first date. In town. Food arriving any second. People who knew them both able to see them. And Noah wanted to answer her.

Honestly. Something he'd yet to do even with his own parents.

And whether it was a good move or not, a relationship

ender before it had even begun or not, he started where it all made sense. "I was destined to be a rancher before I was conceived," he told her. "I can't remember a second of life where I didn't know who I was and what my future would be. Which also happened to be the only thing I wanted it to be…"

"Like I know that no matter what else I choose to do with my life, I want to get married and raise a family here in Tenacity," she said softly, meeting his gaze with understanding, not expectation.

He nodded. "It was all so clear to me, it never dawned on me that it wasn't as clear to everyone who knew me. This is Tenacity. Everyone knows everything about everybody." Or so it seemed.

Her nod, the way she was looking at him, just kept pulling words out from inside him. "I missed a lot of days during high school. The ranch was my future—it came first. And Joanna, she'd been a friend since kindergarten. We'd been king and queen of the seventh grade dance." He offered that with a grin to someone who'd know exactly what he was talking about.

Because Lucy had attended the same school he had and they were *still* holding those awkward opportunities for new teens to get their first taste of dating.

When she grinned back at him, he continued. "When I'd miss school, Joanna would bring me the lessons. Explain what I'd missed. Make sure I had all my homework assignments. She was a whiz in school. Loved learning. And she loved being on the ranch, too. Would come out just to sit on a fence and watch whatever we were doing."

Noah took a breath. Left room for Lucy to intervene. Almost as though she knew he was getting to the messed-up part, she just sat there. Watching him with compassion. But no sign of pity.

"Everyone just accepted that we were an item. That she was happy to be there because she was so in love with me. I bought into the whole idea, too. Thinking, just as I was born to that ranch, the Stargazer, we'd gravitated together because it was the steps we were meant to take."

Lucy took a sip from her drink. She'd glanced at his chin. But she didn't turn away.

He waited until she was looking him in the eye again before he continued. "I knew the truth, though. I mean, I figured the rest was true, too. But Joanna came out to the ranch so much because she craved the peacefulness. The lack of animosity, even when my family members were angry with each other. Her family wasn't that way. At all. They yelled at each other, talked nasty, as much as they talked any other way. Her parents were never physically abusive, but they were volatile. And her siblings, as they grew, were as well. The constant flying off, the lack of anyplace that felt safe from a possible eruption, the constant chaos between everyone in that home was too much for Joanna's spirit."

"And the Stargazer was her refuge," Lucy said softly. "You were her refuge."

He shrugged. Refuge. The word fit. "I wasn't the love of her life," he said. "Nor was she mine." He just hadn't given the matter any thought. What made sense made sense.

"So that's it? You two talk one night and figure out that you aren't deeply in love—" She broke off. Her eyes wide, and filling with something akin to horror. "One of you fell in love with someone else," she guessed.

And Noah wished he could just nod. The solution was so much cleaner. Understandable.

And so, for a second, he did nod. And then said, "I fell in love with Charlie, Henry and Gavin."

Her frown was understandable. To be expected, really. "So?" she asked. "Moms typically expect that to happen…need it to happen…"

And then her brow cleared. "Joanna didn't?"

He shook his head. Then said, "She did. Of course she did." He stopped. Had gotten ahead of himself.

"Being a rancher, running a family ranch, requires having a family," he said then. "To me, that was as obvious as the fact that I'd be around cows and riding horses."

Lucy nodded, her gaze narrowing slightly. Feeling as though she was already getting to his punch line helped drive him there. "Joanna was hesitant about having kids, but eventually agreed to one. To see how we did. I didn't listen to that hesitation. Didn't pursue it. I bowled over it, assuring her over and over how great it was going to be. And she always nodded and gave in."

"Because she'd learned young that speaking up meant starting a war she wasn't emotionally equipped to fight."

Noah stared. Everything around him just seemed to fade away. The delicious aromas, the sounds of diners around them, silverware, clinking glasses, movement. It all just disappeared. His entire world became Lucy for those seconds. Her face. Her words.

But his words, too. Unspoken ones. Just as she'd naturally seemed to understand what his little men needed, she'd seen inside his private hell.

"And I failed to stop long enough to ask questions.

To see that something was wrong. I failed to see her," he said. Not out of any desire for pity. But because the words were his truth. One he was going to have to live with for the rest of his life.

Lucy didn't even blink. Or sit back. She was right there, leaning into him. Her gaze holding his steady, as she said, "And when you found out you were having triplets?"

"Yeah." He nodded. "She tried," he said, swallowing. "She did all the things, did them well, but inside, she was getting tighter and tighter."

"There's no peace with three babies who all have critical needs and only one way to express them—through crying."

That and a million things more. "The boys were about four months old when the screaming started to become an everyday thing," he told her. "Joanna's, not the boys'. Or mine," he had to add.

She nodded, as though letting him know she understood.

So he finished it off. "One night after the babies were asleep, she came and sat by me on the couch. She told me that she just couldn't do it. That she was becoming her parents and she loved our sons too much to risk raising them in a home that was at all like the one in which she'd grown up. She said her worst fear had always been that she, like her siblings, would grow up to be like them, and that was exactly what was happening."

"And that was it?"

He shrugged. "We talked the rest of that night. In between feedings. And watching her with the boys that night—Henry threw up, Charlie had a dirty diaper that messed all the way up his back and all over his crib—she was okay. Because she'd finally spoken up for herself and was getting out. She was heading toward her peace—whatever that might turn out to be. I told her I would do everything I could to help her fly free. Financially as well as legally."

He'd meant to stop there. But had to add, "We'd also both admitted that night, something that I'd only just realized—I can't speak for her on the realizing part—that while we loved each other, we weren't and never had been *in* love."

Lucy sat back then. Not as though she was going away from him. But rather, she was giving them both space to breathe. To recover.

She took a sip of her drink. Smiled at him. He smiled back and sipped his beer.

And Yolanda was there, holding heavy plates with hands covered in hot pads. "I didn't want to interrupt your conversation, so I kept these warm for you," she said, then added, "So be careful, they're hot," as she set them down. "The tortillas are fresh, as are the veggies. Is there anything else I can get you?"

She could have been emptying the dishwasher for all the curiosity she showed. Which was part of what made her such a beloved businesswoman in their small town. Yolanda cared. She also respected everyone's right to their privacy.

Even if they let some of their beans spill in a public restaurant in the middle of town.

As the woman left, Lucy leaned in, grinning, and said, "So I guess we could have chosen a better place for our little chat. You want to take bets on which one of us hears the rumors first?"

"Wouldn't be fair," he told her, grinning back as he opened his napkin on his lap. "I'd win. Because I already know the answer."

Dropping her napkin to her knees, and opening the foil on her tortillas, Lucy asked, "Oh yeah? Who, then?"

"You, of course. I've been divorced for eighteen months and no one has dared let me hear one word about it. You think they're going to start coming to me now?"

"Maybe," she told him. "Because this could be a beginning, not an end, and everyone likes to be at the start of a good piece of juicy gossip."

He chuckled out loud. Shaking his head at her. Just couldn't help himself. The woman was bold. Strong. Unafraid to just get the tough stuff right out there.

And if he wasn't careful, some of her inherent joy might just rub off on him.

Lucy didn't care about the glances following her and Noah out of the restaurant. Didn't give a rip about town gossip.

And hoped that Noah didn't, either.

For the first time in her life she was on a date that felt…completely right. Comfortable, and yet, so incredibly exciting. It seemed like every time the man looked at her, smiled or moved, her body took note. She'd had sex before. She'd never wanted it like she wanted it with Noah.

And even so, the liquid heat building inside her was a small part of her desire to spend more time with the man. Noah seemed to understand her in a way no other guy ever had. Rather than being put off by the fact that she had her life all figured out at such a young age, he completely accepted that she did.

Because he had, too.

As they climbed in his truck to make the short drive back to her parents' place, the ease with which they'd been together over dinner faded. Silence fell again as soon they were cocooned alone together in the darkness.

Bereft beyond what the circumstances should have instigated, she spoke because she had to. "The looks... what people think...it bothers you." Not a judgment, but not a question, either.

His glance in her direction was short, but not at all impersonal. "Not because I care what people think," he said, his tone as personal as it had been over the past hour.

She took an easier breath, but was still frowning as she asked, "What, then?"

"Because I see the truth in what they're probably saying."

Yeah, she'd been afraid of that. Knew what her mother was saying. Had to know how much of it he was believing. "Which is?"

He signaled the turn before her street. "You're at a different place in life. A decade behind me. You've got your whole future wide-open and free ahead of you. Mine's already pretty much set in stone. On top of which, I don't just come with past baggage. I have the challenge of a lifetime, raising three boys all at once, and them coming first in my line-up of responsibilities is not negotiable."

Yeah, that pretty well summed it all up. And pissed her off, too. "So what you're saying is that you don't trust

me to know my own mind? Or is it that, because you
have three adorable little guys on your own, no woman
gets the chance to share the privilege of loving them?
Or just a younger woman who hasn't already failed at a
relationship? Maybe because she knew she hadn't met
anyone good enough to take the risk. And that's a bad
thing, how? I'm a little confused."

He pulled over. The glance he sent her was intense,
glinting under the streetlight.

"What if it's just that I'm an old soul, Noah?" she
asked softly. "Perhaps I was just born that way. Or
maybe it's because I was an only child and my parents
included me in their adult life more than they trailed
around after me in my childhood pursuits. I was attending the Tenacity Quilting Club while I was in elementary school. I heard all the goings on between the
adults in this town when I was at an age when children
are programmed on high gear for learning..." Getting
off topic, she shrugged.

And then, driven by a fear that she could be sitting in
a make-or-break moment before she'd had a chance to
find out what making it would even look like, she said,
"We're on a first date, not planning a future together."
Yet. The word slipped in silently.

Maybe they never would be. It was certainly possible
that she and Noah would find they didn't enjoy spending time together after the newness wore off. She didn't
think so. Not based on the strength of feelings she'd always sought, but never found, suddenly surfacing inside her. But she was old enough to keep that piece of
wisdom to herself.

He wasn't looking at her anymore. Or driving, either. He sat, truck running, but in Park, staring out the front windshield.

Preparing herself to hear that she'd just had her only date with Noah Trent, she said, "Say something."

"What if I need the possibility of planning a future together to be on the table?" He asked the question, glanced at her just as her mouth fell open, and then, shaking his head, said, "Last week I was certain I'd never date again—at least until the boys were self-sufficient—and now a week later, I just said that?" He turned then, pinning her with his expression. "I'm not twenty-four, Lucy. And I have three little guys who are fully dependent on me and are going to be for a long time. I'm not free like you are to casually date, or just have fun for a while. My boys—okay, Charlie—is already asking about you when you aren't there. And I'm pretty sure Henry is, too, and that Gavin would if he was verbal yet. When I see someone, so do the boys..."

His gaze seemed to beseech her to make something right.

She only said, "Are you saying you want to see me?"

He gave her one slow nod.

And Lucy's heart soared.

Chapter Seven

Noah had no idea what was driving him toward the woman. Every logical bone in his body was telling him he had to pack up his tent, go home and stay there. He'd known the woman a matter of weeks. And he was talking about possibilities of a future as a requirement of seeing her again socially?

He'd known Joanna eleven years before they'd even started dating.

And yet, there he sat, truck running, wasting gas, while he opened the door to staking his tent to Lucy's ground. Maybe even cementing the stakes at some point.

He hadn't even told his family he was going out with her. Though, to that point, he was fairly certain they knew. He'd brought her home to share babysitting duties with his mom.

And his mother had had nothing but praise. Only a sentence or two, but that fit. Olive approved of Lucy's care for the triplets.

She wasn't going to give her thirty-four-year-old son dating advice.

Not unless he asked for it.

That was not going to happen.

But apparently going out with Lucy again, was. "You want to go see a movie or something Saturday night?" he asked, feeling about fifteen again.

And not in a good way.

"Assuming one of my sisters, or my parents can watch the boys." He hadn't been to a theater in years. Had no real desire to sit in the dark among strangers for a couple of hours, either. But the drive back and forth, maybe getting something to eat…it was what people did on dates.

"I'd rather hang out at your place, with the boys. Maybe watch a movie or something with you after they're in bed," Lucy said. Staring him right in the eye. "I haven't been to a movie theater in years," she added, as though reading his thoughts and pinning him to the wall with them. "Unless you want to pretend that we're in high school or something," she added with a raise of her brows.

He got her point. Shook his head with a chuckle, and sighed. "You want to change your mind about going out with me again?" he asked, head back against the rest, facing her.

"Nope."

And something in him just couldn't accept grabbing what they both wanted. "I don't get it," he told her. "I can't be the only guy in this town who's asked you out. I mean, have you looked at you? Or talked to you?"

"Every day," she said, without a smile. "And you aren't the only one who's asked me out."

She rattled off a few names. All of which he recognized. Guys who were all younger than he was. Two who were divorced. One of whom had kids.

One, a rodeo rider who seemed to rival Noah's

younger brother Ryder for how many women a guy could get in a month.

Jealousy hit him. Followed by disappointment. For the second it took for him to be happy for her. "You've been out with all them in the few months you've been back in town?"

"Nope, this is my first date in months. Like you, I have no patience for wasting my time on just having fun. It's just never been me. And I know that sounds off-putting, but it's just the way it is. I'm not saying I'd say yes to the first guy who proposed to me. One did and I said no. But when I find the right one, you can bet I will. Marriage is my ultimate dating goal. And if that bothers you, then I guess we need to know that now."

"How do you know these few invites weren't right if you didn't even give them a chance?"

She looked at him for a long time. Whether deciding what to say, or *if* she should say, he couldn't tell. But he waited her out.

She turned her head, facing the windshield, and disappointment hit him again. "Why did you ask me out?" Her question was not at all what he'd been expecting.

Unprepared, his honest answer was out before he'd had a chance to hold back. "I have no idea," he told her. "At least no logical one."

She turned to look at him and he said, "I…feel something…different…when I'm with you."

Her head fell back against the rest, as his had done, but was still turned toward him. "Kind of like a smile inside?" she asked, as though seeking his opinion about the beer he'd had.

With another half chuckle, he reached out to touch

her face with his hand. Almost as though making sure that the surreal moment was really happening. "Kind of," he allowed then.

"Yeah, me, too."

Which made absolutely nothing clear. Except that they were likely going to see each other again. Saturday at his place. With his tribe all over them.

Lucy's glance, even in the dark, offered invitation. One that was too soon for him to accept.

Forcing himself to look away, he put his truck in gear before he got them stuck in something that he couldn't get them out of.

For all her talk of being as mature as any thirty-four-year-old, Lucy felt like she was about seventeen as Noah walked her up to her parents' front door.

"I'm looking at a house," she blurted on their way up the walk. She named the street it was on. "It's only two bedrooms, but would be a good investment. As soon as I get permanent employment, I'm planning to make an offer on it." She was rambling again.

And half watching for the living room curtain to twitch, alerting her to her mother's watchful eye peeking out at them.

Knowing that Noah had to be aware, too. And right back to feeling like he was in the wrong time, but maybe with the right person.

"You're talking about the old Gumser place?" he asked.

She nodded and said, "Yeah." She could have mentioned that she'd been there with her mother once, to visit the older gentleman who'd used to be a schoolteacher in

Bronco and then moved to Tenacity after his wife died—and lived alone for the next thirty years. But didn't.

She was too busy getting ready for Noah's lips on hers. Finally. She'd been imagining his magnetism locking her in since the first day they'd met at Little Cowpokes. Was sooooo ready.

They reached the stoop. Stepped up together. His hand settled on her upper arm. She turned. Felt his other hand gently cup her free arm. Lifted her face up to him. He studied her for a long minute. As though absorbing every inch of her face. Building the anticipation.

And then, with a sigh, he dropped his hands, stepped back down to the sidewalk and said, "I'll see you in the morning."

Disappointment took all the pizazz out of her. She felt like she might cry. From frustration, if nothing else. And then he stopped a few feet away. Spun around, and added, "And...to confirm, Saturday late afternoon and evening at my place, right?"

And just like that she was alight once more.

Noah felt more like himself as he wheeled his little men toward the doorway into Little Cowpokes on Friday morning. He'd just had dinner with a friend. Was having a friend over to spend some fun time with him and the tribe on Saturday. He didn't have to make a world event out of it.

People had friends over all the time. It was what regular folks in regular lives did. He should have done it sooner. Should do it more.

Yeah, maybe he'd do it more.

"MeWoo!" Charlie yelled out so loudly that folks

probably heard him across the street, and Noah took the little guy's exuberance in stride. Same when Henry said, "WooWooWoo!"

He opened the door, pushed his big stroller inside without a hitch.

And then heard, "Ooooo. Ooooo," along with the very distinct sound of one foot picking up and slamming down and then the other.

Glancing up, he saw Lucy coming through the door from the daycare rooms into reception. Saw the way her mouth dropped open, stayed open as she looked up at him. Until she said, "Did Gavin just say my name?"

Noah shook his head. Certain that Gavin hadn't. Except that…had he? The sound…it hadn't been Charlie or Henry. But Gavin only grunted. And cried. And stomped his feet when he was excited or wanted something.

Moving to the side of the stroller, staring in, hearing Charlie and Henry repeat their calls with more force than before, both of them banging back against the stroller in an attempt to break free of their safety straps, Noah reached Gavin just as Lucy did.

"Ooooo. Ooooo," the smallest Trent man said. Reaching one hand toward Lucy.

And with a grin, Noah backed up to tend to Charlie. And then Henry, listening as Lucy said, "Good morning, little sir. Did you sleep good?"

Noah glanced over in time to see his youngest son, clearly a chip off the old block, reaching up to catch a bead in Lucy's hair. Cows again that day.

And to see her lifting the two-year-old into her arms.

"Oooo. Oooo." Gavin said again, and Lucy turned, but not before Noah caught the sheen of tears in her eyes.

Score one for the littlest Trent man.

Gavin had chosen the moment to say his first word. And it hadn't been "dada."

He'd done one better.

He'd shown his somewhat conflicted father just how important Lucy was to their all-male family.

And that mattered way more than what the town might think.

Lucy hated that Friday night's pickups were so busy, everyone scrambling to get off to their weekend plans. Hated that she'd had no time to speak with Noah alone.

Almost as much as it bothered her that she hadn't been able to get Gavin to call her "Oooo," or make any sound other than his normal grunts the entire day.

Not even as the other two had waved goodbye to her.

Then she'd glanced up at Noah, had caught a second of warmth just for her in his gaze, and had practically floated home.

She'd opted to walk, rather than wait for her mother.

Elaina had spent the morning drive in regaling Lucy with various versions of the same facts. Getting involved with the father of triplets was just asking for problems. Potential heartache. Missed opportunities. That added to the spiel she'd had the night before when Elaina had knocked on her door after Lucy had gone up to bed without stopping in the television room to tell her folks good-night. The Thursday night version had been equally potent. Strong reminders that Noah was ten years older than her and divorced. Adding that Viola— one of her mother's friends who'd called after seeing Lucy and Noah at Castillo's that evening—thought Noah was probably looking for someone to take care of his kids. And while no one could blame him, Elaina didn't want that someone to be Lucy. She had a career to pursue. Bigger things than being bogged down all day every day keeping up with another woman's triplet sons.

Elaina hadn't meant to be cruel. Lucy knew that. Understood completely that her mother spoke out of love for her only child, out of worry for things she feared Lucy couldn't see.

Thing was, Lucy saw them all. Recognized the validity in everyone's concerns for her.

But wasn't at all fazed. She and Noah hadn't been looking for each other. They'd just happened to meet. And seemed to fit in the same space.

What that meant in real time, or for the future, she didn't know, but she knew that as long as he was on board, she had to find out.

Noah refused to vacillate on his choice to have Lucy out to his place on Saturday. He'd made the decision, issued the invitation and she'd accepted. The only way it wasn't going to happen was if she backed out.

Maybe because he half thought she might, he didn't tell anyone about the date. He was a grown man. Didn't have to report his guests to his family. His parents had given him his autonomy when he was in high school and started his own small spread on a portion of the family ranch his father had allotted as his.

Refusing to reconsider didn't mean that his conscience left him alone, however. He'd been as culpable as Joanna in the miscommunication that had led to the breakup of their marriage. He'd failed to see where his life plan negatively impacted hers.

No way he could ignore all of the negative impacts inherent in opening the door into his set-in-stone chaotic world to a twenty-four-year-old who had no responsibilities or obligations. Someone who could go wherever, become whatever she wanted to be.

He'd already become. And to invite her in meant loading her down with the responsibility he and Joanna had created.

Of which she was well aware. She'd boldly claimed her right to her own mind and to go after what she most wanted. Hadn't she told him she was interested in pursuing a relationship with him?

With his tribe strapped in their stroller, he pushed it with one hand and the cart with the other up and down the grocery aisles Saturday morning. He'd already laid out some of his own ground beef to thaw, to make sloppy joes for the boys, and—in light of Lucy's disastrous date at the French steak place, where she didn't actually get to taste the steak—he'd also laid out two of his best cuts of filet. And vowed that she would get to the part of the date where she enjoyed Trent Angus, Montana style.

She'd told him Friday afternoon that she'd bring dessert.

Which left potatoes and salad, all the fixings for which he tossed into his cart. Along with half a dozen canisters of the puff treats the boys liked. Another gallon of milk. One of juice for himself. And a case of the boxed juice drinks with straws for the little men.

All three boys reached for various things as he pushed them along, but he'd long since learned how to keep them enough center aisle that they couldn't actually touch. And he never lingered anywhere. He knew what he wanted, grabbed and tossed.

He and the triplets got their usual glances—an occurrence everywhere they went—but folks in Tenacity were understanding enough to let him get on with his business without actually interrupting him with conversation.

And he made it out of the store without a single tear or screaming session. Didn't hurt that he'd given each boy a toddler sucker before they'd entered the store. He had six sticky hands, three sticky faces to wipe before he transferred bodies to car seats—and a stroller to hose off when he got home, but that was a normal day in his world.

In contrast, he spent the drive home imagining what a normal day of shopping would look like for Lucy. And felt again a severe sense of unrest at the idea of invading her freedom with his incredible lack of it. Clicking the steering wheel to turn on the audio that automatically hooked up to his music app, Noah turned up the volume as one of Henry's favorite songs—the shark one—came on, and stole a few quick glances in his rearview mirror to watch his sons as he sang along at the top of his lungs. Gavin's feet moved back and forth, one at a time—in beat with the music. Charlie was waving his arms and belting out his own rendition of the words. And Henry, grinning, had his face turned toward Noah, even though the little guy could only see the side of his face.

Noah was smiling from the inside out as he pulled into Stargazer Ranch and then looped around to head back to his spread. His life wasn't perfect. Or free. Or even easy a lot of the time. But it was filled with love. And, for the most part, made him incredibly happy.

It was a life he wouldn't trade for anything. Not money. Not fame. And most certainly not for his own freedom to go or do. He'd arrived. Was doing.

And had a quickly approaching date with a woman who was putting an excitement in his life he'd never known before.

Chapter Eight

Lucy had a firm talking with herself as she parked her car at the side of Noah's two-story house on Stargazer Ranch. Spending time with Noah, and most particularly with his sons, couldn't be just a good time. She had to keep her eyes wide open. To see the difficulties, not just the joys. To get to know the man inside the hunk cowboy—though she was pretty sure she'd seen a glimpse of the real thing during their conversation at Castillo's and wanted more.

A lot more.

But not unless she would be happy with those three precious little guys when the newness wore off. And she couldn't just walk away.

It wouldn't hurt her life any to play house for a while. But it could devastate theirs a second time were she to be there and then just vanish.

The four Trent men had already been abandoned once. She would not be responsible for it happening to them again.

When Noah had first made the comment Thursday night about looking for long term, she'd been all swoony and thinking of her desire to date him. Excited to know that he was open to seeing where things led.

But he'd been saying something much more than that. He couldn't let his little boys fall in love with a second woman only to have her leave them.

Which meant it was Lucy's job to find out if she was all she thought she was before things went much further.

Quite a feat she'd set for herself.

And yet, as she put her car in Park, she was high on life. Filled with excitement. Happier than she could ever remember being. She wouldn't go so far as to say she felt as though she was coming home, but the idea of doing so, there, at some point, felt more than just thrilling. It felt…right. In a peaceful kind of way.

For some woman.

Maybe her.

Set in front of mountain peak, and angled, the house was in a world of its own. And came with two mangy-looking dogs who were gloriously happy to see her, apparently, based on their exuberant, tail-wagging greeting. One night at pickup Noah had said he had two ranch dogs. Brothers. Jerry and Lewis. Named after the late comedian. Apparently he'd grown up watching old movies of Lewis's as a kid.

"Which one of you is Lewis and who's Jerry?" she asked.

Both of them were mostly black animals and were wagging their tails, but the one who was slightly larger—maybe thirty rather than twenty-five pounds—barked. A happy as opposed to threatening sound. She laughed, bent down to look them both in the eye as she introduced herself to them, and was just standing when Charlie came darting around the side of the house. "Dog! Dog! No! No!" he said, sternly. And then "MeWoo!"

He started to run so fast he tripped over his feet, fell to the ground and, before she could get to him, was back up and running toward her again as Henry came around the corner. "WooWoo!"

The dogs, who were obviously trained to watch out for the boys, not hurt them, backed up, watching. And Lucy, who had laughter bubbling up out of her, was just reaching down to the backs of the two toddlers who each banged full force into a thigh a piece, when Noah—in jeans and a button-down, short-sleeved blue shirt like his sons—came around the corner, carrying Gavin.

"Ooooo," Gavin said, pushing against Noah's chest to get down, and then he came toward her, his arms outstretched.

With the other two boys hanging on to the bottom hems of her black shorts, Lucy bent to pick up Gavin, settling him on her hip with a kiss to his cheek, before meeting Noah's eyes.

"Welcome to the zoo," he said, with a shrug. And a slightly serious depth in his eyes.

And Lucy knew, right then and there, that no matter what happened in the future, whether she ended up with Noah or not, she would always hold that moment dear to her heart.

It was heavenly. Perfect.

Her heart was singing.

And right then, there was nowhere else on earth she'd rather be.

After running the container of homemade cupcakes Lucy had brought into the house, Noah took her and his tribe to his barn, Lewis and Jerry running in front of them, and then circling behind, watching the little guys. Always. Anytime they were around.

He was aware that his gang was excited, needed to expend some energy, and that they'd also be at risk for over-tiring, which would make them cranky—not a pretty sight or sound times three. But he thought he had everything planned to a T, except that with his three, nothing ever went exactly as planned.

The boys loved to sit atop each horse stall, with Noah holding them, to pet Starlight and Gazer—and they had a system. Two of the boys would stay lined up, backs to the wall of the stall, while Noah held the third. It was the law. Only way to get to pet the horses was to stand back to the wall.

But with Lucy there, no one seemed able to contain himself long enough to get his back to the wall. They ran. Henry slid in the hay and fell, screamed at the top of his lungs, and had a bump on his chin. It took some time for Noah to calm him down, and for Lucy, who'd been studying the damaged chin, to announce that no medical attention was needed. Then he turned back to the other two. But they were missing.

Damned rookie mistake. He knew better than to let his eyes off any of them for a second. But with Lucy there...

Running at full speed, Henry still in his arm, he made a full three-sixty around the barn, taking in every visible area on his route. Only to take the last corner and see Lucy standing at the barn door with one of his sons on each hip.

"We played a game of hide-and-seek the other morning in the playroom," she said to him. "The children have rules about where and how they can hide. Always with a partner. And only in play places. Apparently, you let them play in the hay?"

He hadn't checked the hay. Good Lord, what in the hell was wrong with him?

"Unn Unn," Henry said then, emphatically, as he kept pointing toward the other side of the barn.

"Gen," Charlie said then, pushing to get down from Lucy's hold. "Me, turn. Gen," he said. His version of 'again.'

Noah ended up running around the barn with Charlie. And then, of course, with Gavin, before any of them made it inside to pet the horses.

That also had to be different, with Lucy there. He held two while she held one, and all the petting happened at once.

After which, setting Gavin and Charlie down, Noah noticed a big wet splotch all over the side of his shirt. He glanced down at Gavin's jeans to find the matching splotch, from the inner thigh all the way to the hem.

"I've noticed he tends to hold it and let it go all at once," Lucy said, walking up to take Gavin's hand. "Usually I'll check him when I change the other two, and he's dry, and then a little bit later, he's soaked. I'm guessing he's going to be first when it comes to potty training."

Staring at her, Noah thought about the morning weeks before when Gavin had left a few drops in the urinal. And Charlie had wet the floor.

The same had happened several times since. He grinned and reached out to do a fist bump with his youngest son. "Way to go, Gavin!" he said, before picking the little guy up to head to the house.

He was thrilled to think that Gavin, who was behind in everything due to his rough start in life, was finally going to come in first.

And startled to the point of life-changing to realize how incredible it was to have someone there at home with him. Knowing his sons' habits.

Realizing something key about the little men that he hadn't yet figured out.

And acting as though it was all just part of a normal day.

Lucy chose to do the dinner dishes while Noah put the boys to bed. As much as she wanted to be a part of the nightly ritual, since she was there, she knew that some things were sacred. And, with two-year-olds, best left to routine, too.

Had she been babysitting, the situation would be different. The parent wouldn't be there. It was understood that things would be different.

And maybe, just maybe, she needed to hold something back. In case Noah decided that having her around didn't work out well enough for him.

The afternoon had been magical in so many ways. But there'd been almost no personal interaction at all between her and Noah. Understandably, of course, with three overexcited and mobile toddlers on the loose. But there could have been a glance now and then. Something that told her he not only trusted her with his sons, but was enjoying her company himself, too.

Finishing the dishes before Noah had returned, she

moved into the family room in the front of the house, and picked up toys. Lewis and Jerry were out on the ranch, where they lived, running after cows, running off coyotes, and generally having the time of their lives.

Until Noah went to bed. He'd told her one of the first times they'd chatted at Little Cowpokes that while a lot of ranch dogs slept in the barn, he always brought his mutts—as he'd called them—inside at night. She'd have liked their company right then.

She wasn't sure how long Noah wanted her to stay. If he expected her to stay at all. He'd said they'd watch a movie or something after the boys went to bed, when he'd first mentioned the date. But he had given no indication since if he still wanted her to hang around.

"You're still here." His voice startled her. Swinging around, she saw him standing in the doorway, his shoulders looking way too good in the T-shirt he'd pulled on after changing himself and Gavin earlier. The tight cotton hung to just above the midfly on his jeans and she'd been trying not to notice all evening.

Reeling from his words—as though he had expected her to leave without a goodbye?—she was staring at the midspot just because she wasn't ready to look up at him.

She heard him chuckle as he added, "I wouldn't have blamed you if you left a sweet note and ran," he said, coming further into the room.

That was when she noticed that the hand she hadn't seen behind the doorframe was holding two bottles of beer. "It's all I have," he said, holding up one bottle. "You okay to have one and still drive?"

Heart soaring, she smiled as she approached slowly. "Depending on how long I stay, I can have two," she said. "I did the whole test-your-limit thing in high school, where they actually test your blood alcohol level," she said, taking the bottle he opened and handed to her. "I'm one an hour, and still sober to drive. How about you?"

They hadn't had the program yet when he'd been in high school. But his youngest sister, Cassie, had been. And he'd had himself tested just for the hell of it. "Two an hour," he gave her his number. "But with the boys, I don't push that. I'm guessing my endurance has waned some."

Coming more fully into the room, Noah glanced around before slouching down to a corner of the couch. "Wow, this place looks great," he said, holding his opened bottle up to her as he had the other night. She clicked hers against his, then sipped.

And sat down not far from him. It was where she wanted to be.

They were on a date.

Glancing over at him, she said, "I needed something to do." She stopped. Told herself to leave it at that. And then opened her mouth again. "I wasn't sure you wanted me to be here when you came down," she admitted.

His frown was a balm to her ego. "Why would you think that?"

"You've seemed...distant...since not long after I got here."

He shrugged then. Sipped his beer. "Just needing to take things slow," he told her. Then he glanced back over at her. "You know how sometimes when things seem too good to be true, they are?"

Ahhh. The insight set her heart right. "Yeah, and then sometimes you're so busy being afraid they aren't that you don't see when they are."

With another slow nod, he gave a slight grin, leaned his head back against the couch and turned to look at her. "Will they still be good if I say I'd like to just sit with you and watch television?"

Settling back herself, pulling one of the boys' blankets over her bare legs because they were cold, she said, "They'll be better than good."

They chose to stream a crime show they both liked. Lucy sipped her beer until she didn't want anymore, then set it down on the table in front of the couch—one with rubber molding installed all around the edges—and proceeded to fall asleep.

She woke up to see Noah asleep beside her.

She smiled.

And she sat there watching him, as much as the large flat-screen mounted to the wall across from them, until she knew she had to either leave or stay the night.

She was exhausted and she didn't want to fall asleep on the drive into town.

Tiptoeing, she collected her purse, decided to leave the cupcake container, and with a soft kiss to Noah's forehead, she let herself out.

And she was already home, showered and in bed, when her phone vibrated with an incoming text. Switching from the puzzle game she'd been playing in the dark, trying to wind down enough to sleep, she read, You home safe?

Yeah

Sorry I conked out on you

I'm not

Solves 1 wondering

What?

Whether or not there'd be a kiss good-night and how it would be

There was and it was…nice, she typed back.

She was still smiling half an hour later when they finally typed good-night and she curled up with her pillows and pretended they were him as she fell asleep.

She'd kissed him. And he'd slept through it, he reminded himself a few days later when he was out riding the herd.

Nice. She'd said the kiss had been nice. Yeah, that was what a guy wanted to hear about his kissing prowess. It had been a long time. Painfully long. But it wasn't a skill you lost. You either had it or you didn't.

He had it.

Granted, he'd been asleep. But nice? Even unconscious he was a hell of a lot better than nice.

He'd slept through their first kiss. Didn't bode well. The old guy sleeping on the couch while his young, beautiful date made moves on him.

Getting hard while riding Gazer was not a good idea. Noah changed the channel in his mind, focusing instead on the herd he was moving from one portion of land to another, riding the ridge that would keep them corralled. Something he couldn't do with a four-wheeler.

His spread had grown exponentially over the years, providing a solid living for him and the boys.

For a family.

The thought interceded.

He wasn't materially wealthy, but he was materially solid enough to provide a decent house, plenty of food on the table, new clothes, toys, daycare, and still have a little leftover every month. And he had a savings account for emergencies.

That was something he hadn't had at twenty-four. Something most twenty-four-year olds in Tenacity wouldn't be able to offer Lucy.

Lucy.

It all kept coming back to Lucy.

She'd met him and the boys for ice cream in town the day before. Followed by a Sunday afternoon hour in the park.

And she'd been waiting for them at drop-off that morning. With new beads in her braids—black-mangy-mutt heads.

Thing was, as eager as she appeared to be to see them, he and his crew had been just as eager to see her. And her mother and Angela Corey had been out in the reception room, too—separately, but both making an appearance—a first in the weeks that his boys had been attending Little Cowpokes. He'd received their messages loud and clear.

They expected him to be old enough to know better.

But were they right in their thinking?

For some twenty-four-year olds, probably. For some thirty-four-year-olds, too. Taking on triplets was not an

easy feat. And it was one that was going to last forever—
at least in some fashion.

Every stage of growing up was going to hit him times
three. With the terrible twos coming up fast.

His own parents hadn't said a word. And they
wouldn't. No matter what they thought. They'd leave
him to make his choices.

Letting Gazer lead the way, Noah tried to keep his
thoughts strictly on the land he loved.

He had a young rancher from a few small burgs over
coming to look at one of his new bull calves that afternoon. A guy hoping to get started on his own spread.
He'd only been able to make it after work, during the
triplets' dinnertime. Something that happened on schedule, or Noah would be late getting them to bed, which
meant potential trouble getting them out the door to daycare in the morning.

The whole daycare thing, while serving its purpose
perfectly, had created a need for stringent dinner and
getting-up times. Something the boys would need to get
used to before they started school, anyway.

That night presented an issue in that Noah had no idea
how long he'd be tied up with a big first in his new young
customer's life. His mom or one of his sisters would step
in. They always did. But he'd wanted to ask Lucy.

And he knew the boys would want that, too. Not only
would they be pleased to see Lucy at home again, they
minded her better than anyone else. Probably because
she had rules at the daycare that she couldn't budge on.
And they'd learned to respect that.

Whereas around Stargazer Ranch, people tended to

spoil them. Which was fine for grandparents. A privilege even.

But not good on a night when bedtime wasn't negotiable...

With Elaina Bernard and Angela Corey having been minding the space around Lucy, Noah hadn't asked her if she wanted to come out after work. She could feed the boys, and then the two of them could have dinner together. Away from watchful eyes.

The herd started to move, distracting Noah from all thoughts but getting the job done. But an hour later, with his herd where he wanted them, and the gates closed, Noah's first thought was right back to not having asked Lucy to watch the boys that night.

Because...she'd issued a challenge to him the other night. To let her figure out what was best for her.

If he issued the invitation, he went against logic, and the opinions of those who had her back. If he didn't, he let her down.

He had his phone out of his pocket before the thought was complete. He pulled Gazer to a stop and sat there in his saddle, cowboy hat blocking the sun from his screen as he typed a quick text.

Deed done, Noah's mind cleared, and freed him up for the full day of work awaiting him.

Except for the occasional checking of his phone to watch for a reply. In case she had questions. And a wondering or two, if she accepted, about how the night would end.

Damn straight it wouldn't be with him asleep.

Any future kissing that happened between him and Lucy Bernard would take place with him fully conscious.

Chapter Nine

Driving out to Noah's on Monday night, Lucy only had one regret. The jean shorts and T-shirt she'd had on all day, on the floor, with one- and two-year-olds. She'd exchanged the tennis shoes she wore to work for the flip-flops she brought every day in case she wanted to stop in town before heading home. Angela offering to take her mother home since the two of them had a regularly scheduled business meeting after work, had just been a nice quirk of fate.

Had she had her way, she'd have gone home to shower, put on something a bit more sexy, but not only had there not been time, she hadn't wanted to raise any questions were her father to be home. Answers to which would be promptly reported to her mother.

She wasn't going to lie about where she was, if or when she was asked. But neither was she a child who had to report her activities to her folks every hour in the day. Or put herself through having to listen to more warnings.

Or worse, having to endure the silent, worried stares. They left her to fill in the blanks, which then became an unending swirl of possibilities that filled her mind with things that didn't need to be there. Whether the tactic was a diabolical trick, gleaned through motherhood and used purposely by Elaina, or was just the way life worked, she didn't know.

As it was, no one on her end even knew where she was heading. She hadn't seen Noah's text until after her lunch break, out in an empty reception area. She had quickly let him know that she was in. And hadn't heard back from him until after she was back on duty. Which meant no cell phone usage. She'd seen his smile emoji as she'd been heading out to her car. Which had been forty-five minutes after she'd seen him for pickup. The reception area had been full and there'd been no time for any private chatting. His "See ya later" with the warm smile accompanying it had been all she'd needed to light her fire.

And she had hoped her answering look had had some effect on him as well.

Not that she had any chance to find out once she saw him again. His client had arrived early and was standing with Noah, waiting for her to take charge of the littles already set up in their straight row of high chairs, with their finger-food-size chunks of chicken spread on their trays. Along with veggies. Green beans for Gavin. Peas for Charlie. And Henry liked corn. Mix them up and they all three just shook their heads.

A new thing within the last week or two, Noah told her as he headed out the door. They had peaches and cut-up grapes, too.

"Mo!" Charlie exclaimed, before the door had even shut behind his father. The only thing missing from his tray was grapes, and seeing the bunch on the counter

by the cutting board, with a knife, Lucy went to work.
A peace in her heart she'd never known before.

Noah made it back for bedtime. And when he came
back downstairs after tuck-in, found Lucy in the kitchen
chopping grapes of all things. "You don't need to be
doing that," he told her, assuaged with guilt. She was
off work.

And working?

But then, what did he expect her to do, left downstairs
all alone, while he was up being a dad? "You should be
on the couch with your feet up, watching TV."

She shrugged. "I'm not much of a TV watcher," she
told him. And rolling his eyes, he shook his head.

Just as she turned.

Her expression dropped. "What?" she asked. "You
seriously just gave me an eye roll?"

Oh, God. He'd hurt her feelings. "Not you," he said,
moving closer to take her wrists in his hands. He'd been
going for her hands, but one of them still held a knife.
Turning her to face him, he looked her right in the eye
as he said, "It's an eye roll at whatever fates seem to be
firmly pushing me to accept that we fit," he said. He
barreled forth quickly. "I'm not much for TV, either, and
most people are, is all," he told her, hoping the point that
stuck was that they fit.

"You don't want us to fit?" She didn't pull away. Just
looked him straight in the eye with what seemed to him
to be clear expectation of an honest answer.

He gave it to her. "Depends on what part of me you're
asking." He dropped her arms, and leaned back against
the counter.

Lucy went back to chopping, her face mostly hidden by the waves of blond hair falling around her. He homed in on the three thin braids, with black dog-head beads. He'd left Lewis and Jerry outside in the barn. Figured he had another hour, at least, before they came to the back door wanting to be let in for the night.

Wanting the treat he gave them every night for a bedtime snack, more like. And the soft beds by the back door where they slept.

As incredibly intuitive as his dogs were, they weren't going to be able to rescue him from the current situation. It was up to him to do that. The way seemed obvious. "What part of me are you asking?"

Lucy gave him a quick glance, didn't look amused, and went back to chopping. "Why not just introduce me to the various parts and let me hear what each has to say," she suggested, her tone sounding more adultlike than he felt at the moment.

The recommendation seemed fair. Crossing his cowboy booted ankles, along with his arms, he said, "Only two parts. Not various," he started in. "The logical part says the people in this town are wise. Life knowledge learned from hard living. Facing truths. Making smart choices. Logic tells me I screwed up once, do it again, and I'm just a fool."

Her chin jutted. She nodded.

But she didn't turn to rescue him. When he'd gone down a version of that path at dinner the other night, she'd jumped in with counter logic. At least that was how he remembered it going.

"The other part is everything else," he said then. Suddenly he wished he had a beer in his hand, on its way to his mouth. An excuse to not have to say more. Panacea for the sudden awkwardness that was tightening him up inside.

And right then, out of the blue, he remembered being on Gazer's back that morning. Thinking about a second kiss. And said, "The other part is so besotted with my boys I'd die for them," he said. "It soars when I'm out working my spread. And it's so all in to the possibilities you present in my life that I find myself thinking about them—and you—when I'm with my little guys. And out working my ranch."

She turned. Looked at him with glistening eyes, set the knife down, and he was up against her, hauling her against him, planting his lips on hers with a hunger he didn't recognize. Not just kissing her, but tasting her tongue right from the start. Rubbing his jean-clad groin against her jean shorts. Raising his hands to her sides, so that his palms rested against the edge of her breasts.

Her hands planted on his butt, palming him deliciously, pressing him toward her.

And Noah lost all track of logic.

What in the hell was she doing? Egging the man on to drop to the kitchen floor and just do it?

Lucy took a step back, sucking in air. Desperate for something to occupy her hands, other than his hard behind, she reached for a container she'd found in the cupboard earlier, when cleaning up after dinner, and started filling it with the cut grapes.

"We only have professionally sealed toddler fruit cups at Cowpokes," she said, hearing the shake in her voice and taking a deep breath before adding, "Charlie doesn't like them. Bring these grapes in the morning, and I'll make sure he gets them at lunch." Then, hearing herself, detecting a possible back-off in her verbiage, said, "Or better yet, I'll just take them with me tonight, and have them there for him in the morning." She just kept putting grapes in the container with shaking fingers, feeling like the kid everyone in town kept wanting to frame her as.

She'd wanted to be taking responsibility for a little boy that she already loved, and instead, she sounded like she was heading out.

His kiss...she'd never experienced anything even close to it. Had never, ever lost control to the point of her body driving her to get naked on a kitchen floor.

Or just make enough of her accessible to get him inside her.

Her heart was pounding. Desire swirled through her veins. Her panties were damp. Her nipples were throbbing. She was shaking with need. And she had no idea how to appear as though mature sex was normal for her.

"You're heading out, then?" Noah asked, standing right where she'd left him.

She meant to just throw a glance over her shoulder, but when her gaze locked with his, she stayed in the twisted position and asked, "Are you ready to call it a night?"

"Hell no."

She tried to smile then. But the flood of relief that rent through her only lasted the one or two seconds it took for an intense need for sex with him to come flooding back.

Turning back to the counter she found the nerve to say, "Good, because I wasn't planning to head out." She put the lid on the grapes.

And stood there. A mess.

She wanted to be there. Didn't want to be anywhere else. With anyone else. She felt like she just might die if she didn't have sex with him.

And was scared to death that her youth, her inability to control the powerful need swarming within her, was going to convince him to listen to logic.

Or, at the very least, make him desire her less.

She put the grapes in the refrigerator. Left them to whatever fate they might have. Breakfast at home. Little Cowpokes. The garbage after they sat there and spoiled.

Then, gathering herself up as she'd been doing all her life, she straightened her back, held her head high, looked at Noah and said, "Can we talk?"

Can we talk?
Can we talk?
Leading the way into the front room—leading because he was closer to the destination than she was—Noah felt his gut fill with dread.

Can we talk? Ageless words. A version of "We have to talk." And even in a hurting-for-money Podunk town like Tenacity, he'd learned that the general consensus of those words meant some version of "We're through."

Right after a kiss that had him hard as a rock. Painfully pressing against his zipper. Hurting to the point of an inability to speak as he first sat down. To his credit, he'd learned long ago how to ease the malady. He waited a few seconds. Took some breaths. Ran breeds of cattle through his head, along with projected earnings from each bull in the breed.

Whether because she understood his current discomfort, or for some reason of her own that involved not being close to him, Lucy sat a full cushion away from him on the couch.

A very clear step back from Saturday night.

And the complete antithesis to the all-male-driven goal he'd had in the kitchen just minutes ago.

She turned to face him, and his gut sank. It was Joanna all over again. The night she'd told him she had to go. She'd been about that far away. And had turned, just like that, to face him.

With Joanna there'd been relief. A heavy load of guilt. And more relief. With Lucy…the disappointment engulfing him was like some kind of death.

She was playing with one of her braids, running her fingers back and forth across a bead, just as Gavin did. The likeness brought more sadness in its wake.

In just a few short weeks, Lucy had become more of a mothering figure to his sons than his ex-wife had ever been. No fault to Joanna. Just life. And how people were born different. And experiences shaped them.

She'd said she had to talk, but wasn't doing it. He dreaded what she had to say so much, he was fine to wait until they both fell asleep and then woke up at dawn with the boys to get on with the day ahead.

To forget the horror that the evening was becoming.

"It's way too soon for this, but I need to have the 'how many' talk." Lucy's voice, when she'd first started to talk, was like a firecracker shooting through him. He deflected the sting.

Then he heard what she'd said. He had no idea what she was talking about, but was pretty sure it wasn't along the lines of "This isn't going to work."

When you start a sentence with "It's way too soon," that led to a future where it wouldn't be too soon. She wasn't ending them. She was pulling something forward out of their future.

Maybe. Thoughts out of whack, at war with a deflated penis and expectation of an end in sight, Noah glanced over at her. "Come again?"

Nodding, Lucy's look was forthright, as usual, as she said, "I know. Like I said, too soon. But, trust me, I need it."

She needed something. He was happy to give it. Shrugging he said, "The 'how many' talk?"

"Yeah, you know, how many different partners have you had?"

He'd had Joanna. She already knew that.

He was studying Lucy's expression, trying to figure out what she really needed. What he wasn't hearing. Had missed in getting to know her.

Lord knew, his track record with Joanna had shown what a total failure he was in that regard. Didn't surprise him that he was repeating mistakes. Disappointed him, but...

"How many women have you slept with, Noah? How many men have I slept with?"

Oh. Ohhhh. His gaze narrowed as he studied her anew. She was a virgin? His penis leaped at the thought. No...more likely, the opposite. She'd been in the city for six years. Had gone away to college. Had the start of a career. Had dated men who wore black tie and ate French steak. She was trying to tell him that she'd had a lot of sexual experience.

Because...he hadn't done it for her?

She'd certainly responded as though he had. Her nipples had been rock-hard against him. A woman couldn't fake that, could she?

Her gaze was unrelenting. And so he said, "Okay, I've slept with one woman. Now, you go."

He didn't need to know. Didn't think he wanted to know. But the wording of her initial dive into the conversation had been something about him trusting her that she had to have the conversation. And it hit him. Whatever was going on wasn't about him.

Or, at least, maybe about his supposed reaction to what she was about to tell him. What she needed him to hear.

Her eyes were wide, her mouth hanging open. "One?!" She practically squealed the word. "You're the hottest guy in town. As I recall, even as a kid, us girls knew that you were the catch. And you...you only..."

He shrugged. Getting hard at the way she'd just described him. "I told you, Joanna and I were friends since grade school. When kids started dating, we just hooked up as friends. Eventually, we fell into actual dating, and after we graduated, marriage seemed like the next logical step. That was it. One."

"You've been divorced for eighteen months."

He almost rolled his eyes again. Remembered the last time he'd done that he'd hurt her feelings, and said, "You might not have noticed, but I have three very loud, very messy urchins stuck to my skin." And then, more seriously, added, "I'm a single father raising triplets. I haven't had the energy or the desire to pursue a relationship..."

Her face lit up then. "But now you found both?"

His smile was slow, but most definitely there as he said, "It appears that I have."

Chapter Ten

Heart soaring again, Lucy leaned close enough to Noah, reached out to touch the sexy stubble on his chin. Only to have him take hold of her wrist before she got there, and hold her hand away from his face.

Not far away. He didn't return her digits to her physical space. Nor did he allow them their freedom to continue their journey.

"Hold on," he said.

"You said you had to have the conversation. You say. I say," he told her. "'Need' was the word you used, I believe. I gave you my say. You haven't given me yours. Nor have you explained why you needed the information."

The tempered passion simmering in his gaze kind of made her think he was messing with her. The unwavering maintaining of said look gave off a different vibe.

He was actually seeking the answers. And while she'd started out fully intending to divulge her numbers and tell him her reason for asking, she now wanted the whole thing to just go away.

Any further conversation on the matter was going to be embarrassing at least. And could have a much more severe effect on a relationship that promised to stand the test of time if they could just get past the beginning.

Lucy debated leaving her wrist within his grasp, very much wanting the physical connection. But as she formed the words he was seeking, she pulled her hand back. Clasped it with her other one in her lap.

"I've had four," she said, going with facts.

Noah was frowning as he shrugged and said, "Considering that you've been in the city for years, and spent four years at a major university, I would have expected more than that."

Some of the tension suffocating her eased. Not enough, though.

"So what's the problem?" he asked.

With a deep breath, Lucy looked Noah straight in the eye. She'd hoped her reaction to him had been his fault. Because he'd had so much more experience.

And was left to hope that he'd stick by her even if it turned out that, where he was concerned, she was apparently a closet nymphomaniac.

Noah wasn't in a hurry. He was intrigued. And determined to sit there with Lucy until she either told him what was going on or got up to leave. He was laying silent bets with himself which it would be. Talking. Or leaving. He was pretty much landing on a straight fifty-fifty, when she said, "I've been looking for a way to explain my…overexuberance…when it comes to us touching."

Any thoughts of betting pretty much fled as his penis sprang to instant life. "You have," he said, dropping an arm down to shield the evidence of his own…exuberance…until he knew why it was a problem for her.

Her gaze didn't dart from his. Not for a second. His dropped, briefly, to her mouth, when she bit her lower lip. "I'd jumped to the logical conclusion that, being ten years younger than you, I just didn't have your experience, or, rather, enough experience to be with a man who was as capable as you at making a woman feel good. I was afraid I was going to appear too juvenile, and it'd send your concerns about us being together back up to the front of the class."

Funny how she referred to school at the same time she was trying to convince him that he was wrong to question her youth.

Yet, oddly, when it came to sex, their age difference didn't bother him at all. Not only had she been the age of a consenting adult for a lot of years, he also figured that he could make her feel as good as anyone else she might eventually hook up with. Enjoyable sex was something he was confident he could offer her.

Unlike a life that, with him, came with a divorce and triplets on the verge of the terrible twos.

"I make you feel good," he said the words that were forefront in his mind.

She cocked her head, looked to the side, and then back at him. "Do we need to dissect the obvious?"

He thought they should. Just for history, or something. But he found the sense to say, "I'm just wondering why you think that's a bad thing?"

"You make me feel really good."

He shook his head. "Still not getting it." Oh, but other parts of him were. In full force.

"As in, when you touch me, I don't recognize myself," she said, and he had to physically restrain himself from raising his hips in a quest for release.

Or, at the very least, unzipping his fly.

"I feel like this inexperienced maiden who's going to overreact, or hurry too fast, with this hunger that makes me want to get everywhere at once, rather than savoring the moment like a vintner takes his time to inhale, sip slowly, and hold the best wine on his tongue before swallowing. And, all hungry like I am, I'd just tip the bottle, gulp it down like cheap wine, and disappoint you."

Sex talk. She was engaging in mind-blowing foreplay. Understanding hit with a flood of heat that nearly had Noah being done before they'd started.

But when his eyes sought hers, to linger with slow promise of a hunger that didn't disappear after the first swallow, everything stopped for a moment. In her gaze there was not a hint of come-on.

She was being completely serious.

Which kicked his brain into gear. And he wondered, "You're telling me that you've never been turned on to the point of not wanting to stop?" he asked. And might have felt pity for the unknown four men she'd been with, if he hadn't been consumed by tending to her.

"I've actually never been…turned on…so to speak, at all. I mean, sex is fine. After the first awkward time, I didn't hate it. It felt…really good. It's just, you know, something you do to take a relationship to the next level. When you both know that you're ready to pursue the possibility of being…exclusive."

Her words were like a freezing cold shower, outside,

in a blustery Montana January blizzard. What she'd just described...hurt him for her.

"Sex can be that," he told her, holding her gaze. Diving deep within himself, to take the time to know what he was doing and why. And said, "Would it help if I told you that I'm struggling like a horny teenager to control myself, too?"

Her mouth fell open. He didn't budge. Held her gaze steadily.

"So, it's not just me not—"

He lifted a finger to her lips, cutting her off.

She nodded. Still watching him. Then said, "So, maybe it's something else. You know, a mating thing. Nature, interceding to keep us together while we try to navigate our way through a beginning that has some bumps."

He felt some truth in her words. Oddly, in light of his unassuaged earlier discomfort, he found a level of comfort in them.

"Or we could just be hot for each other, and letting it drive us into making the mistake of our lives." He had to put it out there.

Had to be responsible to seeing everything, not just what he wanted to see.

"Maybe." She didn't drop her gaze as she allowed the possibility.

Disappointment sliced through him.

"Are you willing to take that chance?" she asked then, her brow furrowed. "Because I'm not. I'd rather trust that I'm feeling such...powerful...cravings for you because I'm meant to know you better. To be a part of your life somehow. Because the alternative, to put how badly I want to have sex with you down to just…body parts with hormones…seems wrong to me. It's like being given an envelope that could contain a million-dollar bill or a one-dollar bill, and you won't know until you open it. I'd rather open it and take a chance on finding the one-dollar bill, than not and losing the million."

She was killing him. One word at a time. Making him hope. Want.

Encouraging him to reach for something he'd already written off.

She reached out then, touched his chin. And pulled her own hand back. "I fell in love with your sons before I knew how badly I wanted to have sex with you," she confessed. "It's a package deal."

He was.

But she was telling him that she was, too. She was as hot for him as he was for her. But she wasn't going to settle for just sex.

It fit. What she said, what he felt… How could he turn his back on the possibility of finding true happiness? And giving it, too. To her. And to his little guys.

But… "I have a proposal," he said. Only realizing after the word came out that it was the wrong one. "Not marriage," he quickly inserted.

"What's your proposal?"

"I want to open the envelope," he told her. "But not spend the money, yet. Not until we give it a little more time to know whether or not we're holding a one-dollar bill or a million." Her metaphor worked for him. Was logical. He was grasping on to it for all he was worth.

"You want to wait to have sex," she said.

And he had to be honest. "I want to try."

She grinned then. "I'm willing to watch you try."

He wanted to grin back, but couldn't. "I mean what I'm saying, Luce."

She nodded. "I know. And I agree. Completely. I'm just not sure either of us is going to succeed. Earlier, in the kitchen, the only thing that stopped me was my fear of turning you off. Without that, I'm not sure anything would have been strong enough to stop me."

Once again, she was spot-on. And bold enough to put hard truth right out there. With a hint of humor, not panic. Which made him ever more vulnerable to her.

He grinned, then, too. "Temptation's a witch," he agreed. And stood. Held out a hand to her. "It's probably best right now that we say good-night," he said.

Despite his words, he was flooded with disappointment when she stood, gave him a quick, closed mouth kiss on the lips, and, with a saucy smile, let herself out.

Lucy was armed and ready for Noah when he arrived with his crew Tuesday morning. She'd felt his gaze follow her from the doorway to her car, and then out of sight the night before. Had glanced in her rearview mirror just before she turned and lost sight of his house, and he'd still been standing there, in the doorway.

It had taken every ounce of willpower—and a whole lot of determination not to blow their chances for a possible great future together—to keep her foot on the gas. Rather than braking and throwing her car into Reverse.

They were healthy, consenting adults. With an eye on a mutual future. She'd had sex on much less.

And had never wanted it more.

But Noah was right. Incredible passion could be

blinding to other things that would matter more in the long term—and could grow larger than life—if they didn't give themselves the opportunity to find them.

Which was why she told him, as soon as she had Gavin in her arms—and before Charlie was on the loose—that she was going to be attending the Tenacity Quilting Club meeting at the church that night. She'd half thought about going, anyway, as she'd only been a couple of times since she'd been back. But mostly because, for once, Elaina wouldn't be there. She and Lucy's father had plans to play cards with friends who were in town from Bronco that night.

His glance, his raised brow, had told her that he at least suspected she'd blurted her schedule before he could tempt her with another invitation to his spread at Stargazer Ranch. Almost as though he was going to challenge her cowardice.

She'd have admitted he was damn straight about that one, but Charlie was free, running toward the backroom door, and Lucy was busy scooping him up, and then distracting him long enough to get Henry with them, before she'd thrown their father a smile and headed into the day.

And while she'd managed to hold temptation at bay with her absence from his presence for the evening, he and his three littles were on her mind constantly. Almost as though they were already her family, and having them going on with dinner and bedtime without her seemed...wrong. Like she was missing out on a vital part of their lives.

Sitting in the large, fluorescent-lit basement of the Goodness & Mercy Nondenominational Church, she didn't feel as much like she was surrounded by family as she always had. Having attended meetings of the quilting club since she'd been a little girl sitting by her mother's side, that realization struck noticeably. It wasn't so much that she didn't belong there. But that she belonged someplace else more.

She'd known most of the faces her whole life. And yet her heart was telling her that home lay with a man she'd only known a few weeks.

Almost as though she'd been reading Lucy's mind, Winona Cobbs-Sanchez—Lucy's secret ninety-something-year-old girl crush—called out to her. By name.

"I've heard the rumors going around about you and the oldest Trent boy, my dear," Winona said from across the table and down a few seats. "And I must say, you're putting off a completely different aura than I've felt since you came home. I see a halo of light glowing around you."

Going through the fabric she was stitching with more force and less finesse than required, Lucy stabbed her finger. Saw a spot of blood. She did not want to get it on the cloth book she was making for Charlie, but she needed to keep sewing. To smile and laugh off the remarks. Folding her throbbing finger up into her palm, she kept moving her needle in and out, pulling up and repeating the process. A smile on her lips, she said, "We're just friends." In a tone she hoped was nonchalant.

Not at all indicative of the hot and shaky way she felt.

The cloth books—her mother had been making them for the church nursery. No one had to know that Lucy had recently ordered the square fabric story pieces herself online—three different stories geared to three very different little boys—and was not sewing for the church that night.

"He's definitely a treat to look at," Nina Sanchez, a rancher like Noah, said. Lucy glanced up to catch a somewhat doubtful glance from the twenty-nine-year old's striking brown eyes as she said, "But triplets! That's a lot whole lot of diapers."

Pulling her eye back to her sewing after that glance, Lucy filled with an instant of defensiveness on Noah's behalf, quickly gone, but not before she said, "They're in pull-up disposable diapers now." And then, feeling the whole room full of eyes on her as the place went unusually silent, she made a quick glance around and said, "The triplets are at the daycare five days a week." As a way to explain her intimate knowledge of their bathroom progression.

"Noah's such a good man," Winona said then. "I heard he helped that ex-wife of his, Joanna, get a new start. Made the divorce like a birthday party for her. Full of good wishes and presents by way of no financial burden."

The older woman's voice was strong enough to be heard all over the basement, in spite of her years.

Helped along, most likely, by the silence.

Cecil Brewster, the elderly, curmudgeonly rancher who'd recently become the only man to join the quilting club, harrumphed as he painstakingly worked on a quilt square. Not much different than fixing up a saddle, or putting a ripped cowboy hat back together, he'd said when he'd first joined them.

"You got something to say, old man?" Winona continued to hold the conversation as if it belonged to her. "Speak up."

"What kind of woman leaves her husband alone with three little ones to raise?" the man asked, with another snort-like sound.

"She came from a rough home," Angela Corey spoke up then. "I knew those kids growing up. Took care of 'em. Lots of yelling in that house. Constant verbal sparring. Poor Joanna, used to hide herself in books. She'd be shaking sometimes after getting out of the car to come into Little Cowpokes. Girl's got a good heart. And an overload of anxiety, if you ask me. From what I heard, once those three darlings came, the constant chaos was more than she could handle."

"Still, Lucy's only twenty-four," Ellen Cooper, Mike Cooper's mom, said. "You really need to think about the long term, tying yourself down to three children at once," she said. "Mike adores Cody, as do Larry and I, but it changes your life taking on someone else's child."

Lucy remembered Maggie, Mike's twin sister, had left her son with Mike while she was working overseas. They'd been four years older than her, though, so she'd never really associated with them much. "I raised twins," Ellen continued, paying attention to the knitting in her hand as she spoke. "And that was hard. Especially when they're little like that. But three of them!"

Messing up a stitch, making it noticeably uneven, Lucy unthreaded her needle and pulled out the mistake. She contemplated getting up and walking out, rather than rethreading. Maybe going for a walk in the park. Except that she didn't like to do that alone in the dark. Tenacity was safe, but living in the city had instilled a societal caution in Lucy she hadn't yet been able to shake.

However, she *could* shake up the conversation. And knew exactly how to do it. Sending a silent apology to Nina Sanchez—one she hoped Winona didn't intercept and rightly figure out Lucy was purposely deflecting—she said, "Like I said, Noah and I are just friends. And by the way, I heard at the daycare today that Barrett Deroy might be coming back to town next month."

It was cowardly of her, throwing out an obvious attention hooker, but sometimes when family got a little too nosy, one had to do what one had to do.

"Barrett?" Ellen Cooper exclaimed. "He was such a nice kid back in the day."

"Right until he wasn't," Cecil muttered. "Like the rest of 'em. Seemed nice 'til they up and left and suddenly the town's out of money. Seems pretty clear who took it. Been fifteen years. Can't figure why he'd be showin' his face back here now."

"Nothing was ever proven," Nina spoke up, casting Lucy a look that shamed her a bit for bringing up the subject. Nina had had a thing for Barrett. Some said she'd never gotten over it.

Telling herself she'd do something nice for the woman first chance she got, Lucy exhaled. Glad that they'd all forgotten about her love life.

For the moment.

She had a suddenly very acute understanding of Noah's discomfort regarding his and Lucy's relationship. She came out the poor thing being taken advantage of. In some minds, he came out the bad guy.

It was unfortunate. And not appropriate. But in a

small town, it was what it was. She'd wanted to come home. To be where everyone knew everyone else. Watched out for each other.

And she still wanted that.

Which meant that she had to get a thicker skin when her life choices took her against the grain. Because she darn sure wasn't going to stop listening to her own heart and mind and making the decisions that were right for her.

Most definitely when it came to Noah and his sons.

They were becoming a family. A bond that the good people of Tenacity would recognize in time. Until then, it was up to her and Noah to see and hold on to their truth, to endure the bad with the great, and to not let anything stop them from building their lifetime of love.

Chapter Eleven

All three of his little men were in moods Wednesday night. Probably feeding off from Noah. He'd had a hard time not making up some work excuse for Lucy to drive out to the ranch again, as she'd done on Monday. Tuesday had been empty without her. Which he knew, logically, was ludicrous. Two years of one way, versus two days of another, and the two-day way was the one that felt right?

He had very deliberately said a casual good-night to her at pickup that evening. She'd texted him when she'd arrived home the night before. Told him a little bit about the conversation she'd endured. Mostly she'd left him to fill in the blanks.

He'd done a damned fine job of it and hated that he was responsible for putting her in that position. The problem wasn't about her choice to date someone. It was his life choices, his mistakes and his current circumstances that were the cause of all the angst.

The current night's trouble had actually started in the lobby of Little Cowpokes. Gavin had fussed and held on to Lucy's neck, when she'd tried to load him in the stroller. Noah had quickly taken over. Said his quick goodbye, and started to push his way out the door, when Charlie started in with, "MeWoo! MeWoo!"

At which time Henry chimed in with "Woooo! Woooo!"

And Gavin started with a series of half-tearful, "Oooo Oooo Oooo."

Noah didn't look back. Had no idea if Lucy was aware of the debacle on his hands. But he half hoped she was. That she'd see what was really in store when you took on three little ones at once. And run as fast as she could in the other direction.

He adored his little men. Would give up his life for any of them. And there were times when even he struggled to remain calm and loving when they all got going at once.

Dinner was no better.

Charlie, Noah's small leader, started it. "No!" he said when Noah put cut up macaroni and cheese on his tray. Then proceeded to push the pasta over the edge of the tray and onto the floor. By the time Noah saw what was happening, he'd put a pile in front of Henry, who, watching his older brother, picked up a piece of macaroni and threw it, hitting Gavin on the side of the head.

Lifting a hand, Gavin found the cheesy substance stuck to his head and smeared it into his ear.

Things went downhill from there. Noah ended up having to trace his steps to several months back, sitting himself in the middle of the three chairs, with jarred baby food—some kind of stew—and go down the row, hand-feeding each mouth.

Gavin wouldn't eat until Noah gave him a piece of bread to hold. And even then, his littlest guy barely took a few bites. Reigniting concern that had been a constant when his babies had been preemies, and then for months afterward when newborn Gavin wasn't gaining weight like the other two.

After dinner—cleanup of which Noah just left for later—he took the boys into the front room for a toddler show and quiet play, and the first thing Charlie did was snatch a book out of Henry's hands. Henry let out a wail that could probably be heard at his parents' house, and lifted an arm to hit his brother.

Gavin walked up and got hit instead, just as Noah was reaching for Henry's hand, trying to stop it midflight.

Without a word, Noah pulled the three fur-and-foam armchairs—identical to the ones at his mother's house—and lined them up along the front of the couch.

"Sit," was all he said.

Gavin and Henry sat on command, but Charlie continued to pull books off the shelf, loading up his arms.

Leaving his eldest son to struggle with his load for a second, Noah wiped Henry's hands and face before he ended up with snot on fur, and possibly on his brother as well. By the time he turned back to Charlie, the precocious boy had planted his books on the couch and then, using his chair, was climbing up to join them.

Very deliberately not following his rules.

As tempted as he was to just let Charlie have his way, Noah knew that doing so once could mean havoc for the foreseeable future. Grabbing the boy around the waist with one arm, he lifted Charlie against him. Gave the boy a snuggle of whiskers against the tender neck, and then set him firmly in his chair.

Whether Charlie was just getting tired, or recognized

that he'd pushed Noah as far as he was going to get away with that night, the boy stayed seated. But said, "MeWoo read."

"Wooo. Wooo," Henry yelled to the air in general.

And Gavin…just sat there. Staring at his son, Noah thought the tiny cheeks looked flushed, and assuring himself he was overreacting, he moved over to feel Gavin's cheeks.

They were burning hot to his touch.

Noah remembered how Lucy had remained calm that time in the barn with the boys, the placid way she'd handled the fallen child and then two missing boys. It settled him as he went for the thermometer.

And helped ease the sick feeling in his gut when he read the results. *Not again.* The thought pressed through. *Lucy* came next. From day one she'd been the calm in his storm.

She'd want to know that Gavin was sick.

Probably as much as he wanted her to know.

And because he didn't have the energy to fight fate on two sides that night—the fates that continued to challenge Gavin and the ones that were calling out to Noah and Lucy to be together in spite of all the reasons they shouldn't be—he tended to the one that was the most urgent.

The one that he would always have to tend to first. His son.

Noah called his parents and Cassie to come immediately to stay with Charlie and Henry, and then, loading an eerily quiet Gavin into his car seat, he sped out of the Stargazer, already getting Lucy on the truck's audio system.

In that moment, she was the source of his calm. He needed her.

And Gavin needed him.

Lucy was heading into the Tenacity Social Club on Wednesday night, needing to claim a life of her own after Noah's response to "them" in the daycare that afternoon. She never should have told him about the gossip at the quilting club.

She had just wanted to let him know that she understood his position more clearly, but that the opinion of others hadn't swayed her in the least to the rightness of them being together.

She'd thought they were a united team when she'd hung up. Not so that afternoon. What had changed, she had no idea. Because Noah hadn't shared his thoughts with her. His choice to be that way.

But without the vital communication staying open between them, they had little chance of finding the happiness she knew in her heart was waiting for them.

Yet...if it wasn't in his heart...

Her cell phone rang just as she was reaching for the door of the club. Stepping back away, she glanced at the phone's screen and was already heading back to her car when she heard Noah say, "Gavin's spiking a fever. I'm on my way to urgent care, East Montana UC in Mason Springs. I thought you'd want to know."

He didn't sound at all like the calm, easygoing man she knew him to be. "What's wrong?"

"I have no idea," he told her. "Did he have an appetite at lunch?"

She climbed in her car. "Same as always. Though he

was a little clingy after that…wanting me to hold him." Oh, God. Had she missed a sign of something amiss? Something a mother would have automatically caught? "I'm so sorry, Noah, I didn't—"

"I didn't, either," he cut her off. "Not even when he didn't eat much of his dinner. Based on the past, it's likely that it came on suddenly. I left Charlie and Henry home with my parents."

Car started, she pulled out onto a thankfully deserted road. "I'll go out and sit with them," she said, already heading that way.

"Actually," his tone had changed, softened with the word. Nothing else came with it.

"Actually what?" Was he going to tell her it was best that they go their own ways? Had he only called to let her know the boys wouldn't be at Little Cowpokes the next day? And there she was playing house and rushing off to help?

Even if he was, she wanted to help. Her heart was with them whether Noah was able to accept it or not.

"I was hoping you'd meet me at urgent care," he said, taking her breath away. "I know it's a lot to ask, but Cassie's with Mom and Dad, and… I…it was like this a lot when Gavin was little," he said. "I just…we'd do better if you were there."

Squealing her tires as she made the hurried, tight, illegal U-turn, Lucy said, "I'm on my way." Completely focused and serious, she kept Noah on the phone, hearing that Gavin had fallen asleep and all about the disaster dinner had been that night, until he'd arrived safely at the medical facility and had been whisked immediately into an examination room.

* * *

Gavin didn't wake up. Other than brief moments, when he was moved or fussed with, he never opened his eyes. The room was small, far too quiet, and filled with all kinds of medical equipment that induced difficult memories.

Noah was losing his battle with helplessness-induced panic when he saw Lucy's text that she'd arrived. Not wanting to leave his ailing boy, even for a second, he asked an aide to bring Lucy back to their private room, and stood in the doorway, waiting for the sight of her.

In jeans and a ribbed, form-fitting, short-sleeved black shirt, with black wedge-heeled sandals, she looked like...hope.

The sensation hit him. Filled him. Drowning out the anxiety that had struck him when he'd read the thermometer in his living room.

His son had a fever. Toddlers got them.

Her smile flashed briefly, a hello that soothed the beast of worry inside him. "How is he?" she asked softly, her brow furrowed as she drew closer to the bed.

"He was at 104.5. They've given him a fever reducer and taken blood. He's been asleep the whole time, other than waking briefly when I pulled him out of the car, and when the doctor purposely rattled him to make sure he could get him to consciousness."

"He sleeps through a roomful of kids playing and screaming," Lucy said then, still watching Gavin. "I put it down to being in a womb with two other babies. And going through life with them, too."

Laying a hand gently against the toddler's splotched cheek, she leaned down, kissed that same hot skin, and then moved back to sit in one of the two chairs at the side of the gurney.

"What do they think it is?"

The sixty-million-dollar question. One Noah had learned to quit asking. "They won't know anything until they get the blood work back. And see how his temp responds to the medication." He knew the ropes far too well. "It could be anything from basic flu—though you'd think the other two would be showing some symptoms as well if that was the case..."

And there he went. Letting his head get the better of him. Because he'd traveled that road for too long. Mostly alone.

He knew too much. Without knowing enough.

"From basic flu to what?" Lucy asked, glancing briefly at Noah, but keeping her focus on Gavin.

"You don't want to know," Noah told her. More like, he didn't want to say.

Lucy's hand slid over on top of his. Giving it a squeeze. And she said softly, "I do want to know, Noah. Please. You asked me to come. Don't shut me out."

Turning his head, he saw the concern, the depth of compassion in her beautiful blue eyes, and found himself reliving a horror that he'd spent the past year and a half trying to forget.

The fear and frustration. The helplessness. A strong man unable to do a damned thing to help his own tiny son. Except be there. Talk to him. Hoping that messages of strength and love got through even though he'd been too young to understand them.

It was all back.

With a difference.

He wasn't sitting alone in the worried loved-one section of that medical room.

Noah got up, leaned over the rail of the exam bed, touched his son's forehead and sat back down. Lucy held on to the fact that he'd called her. Whether he talked to her or not, he'd wanted her there with him. With them.

Her job was to support. Not push. The feeling on that one was crystal clear.

Noah sat back down beside her. Sighed. And still watching his son, said, "The list of what could be going on with that little man is endless."

She supposed, if you considered every ailment that any child had ever suffered, his statement could be meant literally. But she got the feeling that Noah wasn't talking about any child. Or the world's ailments.

And she waited.

"I'm sorry," he said then, his face turned toward his son, not her. "Just…the whole medical thing…brings back some pretty traumatic memories."

She'd figured. "Because?"

"The little guys were born one day shy of thirty weeks. All of them had to be incubated. The amount of tubes and machines in use for one tiny body…" As her heart pumped harder at the fear he invoked, he shook his head. "Charlie and Henry did pretty well, right from the start. Charlie was four pounds, Henry over three. But Gavin, he clearly hadn't had equal share of the womb. He was just over two pounds. He was in the hospital for a couple of months."

She gasped. Couldn't help it. She'd had no idea at all.

"They've all three been doing great since then, but

I just can't shake the fear, in the back of my mind, that there could be some lasting effects from the early delivery. You know, something that shows up later. Especially with little Gav."

Lucy had never seen Noah so vulnerable. The hunky never-let-them-see-you-sweat cowboy's suffering hurt her heart. She took his hand. Held on tight. Needing him to know he wasn't alone.

"Those first days with Gavin, they all ran together," Noah said then. "I couldn't even hold him. He was in this small crib thing they call an Isolette, essentially tiny baby isolation. The whole thing is encased in plastic. They regulate temperature to keep the baby warm. And it keeps out germs. Emulating the mother's womb, somewhat. They were afraid of infection." He stopped, glanced over at her, and said, "At that point, even the sniffles could have killed him."

She squeezed his hand again and said, "He's clearly got his father's determination. He fought and won."

Noah nodded. Looked back at Gavin and said, "I remember the first time I held him... There were still tubes and he was just wrapped in blankets, no diaper. He fit in one hand." He held up his free hand. Turned it around, looking at it. "I'd been holding the other two for weeks. They were incredibly small, too, but Gavin... I was ecstatic to finally have him up against me. And scared as hell for him, too. There was so much that could go wrong..."

His words dropped off, and afraid Noah was sinking back to his personal hell, she asked, "Was their mother there?" More to get his mind off from Gavin's medical condition at that moment than anything else.

Leaning in toward the emergency room bed, elbows on his knees, and taking Lucy's hand with him, he said, "Yeah. But we were rarely in the same place at the same time. With all three of the babies at different stages, and exhibiting different needs, we had to tag team everything. The whole time they were in the hospital, Joanna was visiting the babies in their different rooms, on a regular basis, keeping track of the differing medications, feeding schedules, needs of each boy. Charting them, almost like a doctor would. She kept a rigid schedule to be there for them as they needed her."

Although Lucy felt the pang of not having had the privilege of being there herself, she was immensely relieved to know that Joanna had been.

"But she was also relieved when she could leave them to their medical teams and go home to the ranch," Noah added. "I couldn't do that. Especially not in the early days. I'd go home to shower as necessary, but spent most nights at the hospital alone with them. Or in a room in a B&B right close. Healing isn't all about medicine and procedures. It's been proven that a parent's voice—something babies recognize from their time in the womb—and the constant outpouring of love from the same people every day, go a long way in the growing and developing process. Hospital staff members care, but they're there a few days and then gone a few."

Blinking back tears that were putting up one hell of a fight, Lucy swallowed hard. Hating that Noah, who was one of the strongest, most responsible people she'd ever known, had had to endure those long nights all alone.

Or at all.

She could hardly bear to think of the danger little Gavin had been in. And Charlie and Henry, too.

"The older two were able to suck pretty soon after birth," Noah said then. "Gavin's muscles hadn't developed enough for sucking or swallowing. He had to be tube-fed for almost a month."

A tear dropped as she looked over at the sleeping boy. She wiped it away, but another followed. She'd held him just that afternoon. Needed so badly to be able to scoop him up and keep him close to her heart. Shield him from whatever battles might lie before him.

And she had to say, "He's going to be okay." The words instilling strength within her. "He came through all that—he's not going to let a fever keep him down," she continued, squeezing Noah's hand again. "Gavin might be small, but he's mighty. In case you haven't noticed, he's got those around him wrapped around his little finger, and manages to get everything he needs to keep him happy."

Noah looked over at her, a slow grin forming on his face. "The first time he had a taste of baby food in his mouth, he kind of froze, and stared...like he had no idea what was happening. And then started to kick his legs, fiercely, making it very clear he wanted more."

Over an hour passed as they sat there, Lucy asking questions now and then, but mostly with Noah just sharing memories as they came to him. The great strides Charlie and Henry took, almost from the beginning. Which also highlighted those Gavin wasn't taking, which made it harder sometimes to see the smaller progress as huge victories, too. He remembered, in detail, the first time each of his boys had smiled at him. Figuring they'd had gas, but the cause hadn't fazed him a bit.

A nurse came in a couple of times to check on them. And to take Gavin's temperature again. It was coming down. Slowly. But responding to medication.

Lucy asked as many questions as he did, only to feel immediately self-conscious in the way she was overstepping. "I'm sorry about that," she told Noah as the nurse left. "It's not my place to take over the conversation." She'd just jumped right in.

A tendency she'd had much of her life, but had thought she had under better control.

Noah picked up her hand again. "Are you kidding?" he asked. "In the first place, the boys are in your care more awake hours on most days than they are in mine. And the second...you have no idea how important that was. To have someone else right here, who's invested in my little guys, thinking of their needs, having my back when there's something I hadn't thought of..."

His voice trailed off, but his gaze remained glued to hers, telling her how much her presence in that room mattered—giving her the feeling that she'd been the wife and mother for a tough moment, and Lucy figured right then was when she fell completely in love with the man.

Chapter Twelve

Noah could hardly believe it had happened, but without knowing anything new—other than fever medication working slowly—he felt far better than he had before in a medical situation with one of his kids. Stronger. More equipped to take on whatever battle was put before them, and come out victorious.

And still he nearly wept with relief when the doctor came to tell them that Gavin's blood work had all come back normal. He had an ear infection that would likely clear up with the antibiotics being prescribed. They were to give him an over-the-counter children's fever reducer and keep a close watch over the next few days, but he was expected to be just fine.

"A bit grumpy, maybe," the doctor said from the doorway, as he left to get the instructional information he'd be sending home with them.

The second the door shut behind him Lucy threw her arms around Noah. Holding on tight. And he squeezed her right back, and spoke softly, right by her ear. "You have no idea how much your being here mattered." In that moment, he could have told her he loved her.

But didn't. Caution still had a hold on him. Rightfully so.

Pulling back from her he said, "Thank you for coming. I know you have to work in the morning..." He'd already said he wasn't going to be bringing the boys into Little Cowpokes the next day.

"I'm coming home with you," Lucy said. "Following you home, since it's late and dark out," she added. "Little ones sense when something is off in their worlds, and if Charlie or Henry wake up, they'll need full attention, and I know you want to keep an eye on Gavin."

The doctor had recommended that Noah check the toddler's temperature every couple of hours that night. Just to be safe.

Even if he hadn't, Noah didn't have it in him right then to tell Lucy no. Even knowing that his mother, who'd stayed at his place with the boys after they were asleep, and could have stayed all night, would know that Lucy was there.

And staying.

To help with the boys only, of course.

But still staying.

Noah needed to be bothered by that, but he wasn't.

Not as he kept both his sleeping son and the car following right behind him in sight via his rearview mirror during the entire drive back to the ranch.

Nor when Olive mentioned that she was fine to stay if Lucy needed to get back.

He'd let his mother know that Lucy had already offered to spend the night. To be there with Charlie and Henry. Just in case.

Lucy might not ever be his wife. But, for the moment at least, she was a vital part of his family.

And he was going to treat her with the respect such a position deserved.

* * *

Gavin whimpered as Noah carried him into the house. But, as he had when leaving the hospital, the toddler snuggled his head against Noah's shoulder and settled back to sleep.

Not wanting him in his toddler bed in the nursery with his brothers, he transferred Gavin to Lucy and went for one of the three portable cribs he kept folded in the hall closet.

Sitting on the couch with the sleeping little boy snuggled up against her, his face cradled up by her neck, Lucy knew a sense of completeness she'd never imagined. Finally holding that little body close, after having had to sit and watch him sleep while they awaited results, she relaxed. Breathed. Blinked back a few more tears.

Took him on as a part of her life. A part of her.

Fully aware that she wasn't just committing to one, but to three. And she was certain that she was on the path her life had been meant to take.

The path she'd come home to find.

Her heart soared as she watched Noah's lithe, strong body make light and quick work of setting up the crib. He was the man in her life.

There were no doubts.

And when he approached, took Gavin from her to lay the little boy down, she went immediately to check on the other two sleeping Trents, and then out to the kitchen. To open a can of beer and fill two glasses half-full.

Just enough to take the edge off a difficult night.

Not enough to impair either one of them.

She held her glass up to clink his—as he'd established as their way—and sat down with him on the couch. They'd had a rough night. But the doctor's news had been great. The other two were sleeping soundly, as usual. Life was good.

"Thank you," he said softly as he touched his glass to hers.

She nodded. Sipped. Laid her head back against the couch cushion. Feeling happy.

Purely, completely happy.

The feeling stayed with her as they talked some, but mostly rested in between checking Gavin's temperature. And changing him, and the sheet and mattress when he wet himself clear through. They worked together as though they'd been through the routine together uncountable times.

And the silences were comfortable, too.

Even when, sometime just after dawn, she awoke to find Noah's arm around her and her head on his chest, she felt more right, than odd.

This is where I belong. The thought came to her along with consciousness. And as much as she didn't want to move, she knew she had to.

She was expected at the daycare. Had to get home and shower. Have a stiff cup of coffee.

Managing to slip away from Noah without waking him, she scribbled a quick note, left it where he'd see it on the table, and tiptoed out.

Noah heard her go. Along with Lewis and Jerry, who'd been left to sleep outside in the barn the night before. They wanted in for breakfast.

Taking a minute to get himself straight, he squatted between the two mutts, scratching them both behind the ears as they liked. Telling them what good boys they were. Asking about their night out.

And then, he fed them both.

Unable to distract himself any longer from the fact that Lucy had snuck out without so much as a goodbye.

Had she awoken with second thoughts about her deepening involvement with his crew? He sure wouldn't blame her if she had. He was thinking about how he'd offer her an out, rather than making her bring it to him, when he saw the piece of purple paper on the kitchen table.

He had no purple paper. But had seen a glimpse of a little pad like that in her purse.

You were sleeping so peacefully I didn't want to wake you. Please text Gavin's temp and overall condition when he wakes up. L.

That was it. Just *L.*

He liked the familiarity of it. The general feel of confidence her words conveyed. As though they were already embarking on a lifetime.

He could hardly keep the door open for her to discover that she needed to move on if he told her that she might just get the lifetime. She needed time to see what she was really getting into before he put pressure on her. Or added his own feelings, wants, burgeoning hopes to the mix.

But before he went for a quick shower, before the tribe was conscious and on the warpath, he took another long glance at Gavin's cheeks, assured himself there really weren't any red splotches at all, touched the skin lightly with the back of his hand, used the ear thermometer to check his temp, and texted Lucy.

Gav's skin is cool to the touch. Color good. Normal temp. Still asleep, he typed and hit Send.

He might not feel the right to pull her any further in, but he damn sure wasn't going to push her out, either. She'd asked for updates, and she was going to get them.

And anything else she needed from him.

Except sex. Of course.

They had their plan, and it was good.

Lucy hadn't heard from Noah by the time she got home. Pulling out her phone, just to make sure its automatic connection to her car's audio system hadn't been inadvertently disconnected, she noticed, instead, that the battery was dead.

She'd completely forgotten about charging it. Would do so as soon as she got inside. Before she showered. She needed to know how Gavin was doing. Had hated leaving before he'd had his temperature taken.

Letting herself in quietly so as to not disturb her parents, she tiptoed through the mudroom into the kitchen, only to stop at the sight of her mother, looking kind of haggard in her robe—her hair all askew as though she'd been running her fingers through it. A cup of coffee in front of her.

The look of sheer disappointment she saw gazing at her from her mother's eyes was not something she'd ever seen before. Not directed at her.

Elaina had been Lucy's biggest champion her entire life.

"What's wrong?" she asked, putting her purse on the

counter, hoping she was reading her mother's feelings wrong. Preparing for the worst without any idea what that would be.

"You leave here early in the evening, without saying where you're going. Or leaving a note. And then you don't come home? What do you think is the matter?"

Taking a step forward, suddenly needing a lethally strong cup of coffee herself, Lucy opened her mouth to speak, but Elaina cut her off with, "I was worried sick, imagining all kinds of things that you read about in the news that happen to young women out on their own..."

Swallowing, Lucy took another step forward. Feeling like she needed to give her mother a hug, or something.

"Why didn't you at least answer your phone?" Elaina asked then. "If Noah has you this tangled up that you forget the basic respect and consideration due to those who live with you..."

Pulling out her phone, she set it on the counter in front of Elaina. "I'm sorry, Mama," she said, a title from her childhood slipping out. "My phone was dead and I didn't know it until a couple of minutes ago. I absolutely would have answered." And then rushed on with, "I was on my way into the Social Club when Noah phoned. He was rushing Gavin to urgent care and asked if I'd meet him there. We sat in a small room, watching Gavin sleep until almost midnight, when the doctor said it was safe to take Gavin home. I followed Noah to his place, and spent the night on his couch, with Gavin in a portable crib a few feet away."

There was a lot she hadn't said. Like why she hadn't thought to call her folks when she'd first heard from Noah. Nor why, with Noah's whole family on the ranch, she'd thought it necessary to follow him home and spend the night.

Elaina's expression softened. With compassion. And it looked like a bit of shame, too. That look pulled the next words out of Lucy. "I'm really sorry I worried you. I hate that you had a hard night because of me. And... I'm an adult, Mom. I've been on my own for the last six years. I truly didn't think you'd do anything other than trust that I was fine. Just like you have the whole time I was in Bronco."

With a nod, Elaina's face softened further, and she gave a small smile as she said, "I guess since you came home I've kind of reverted back to when you were in high school, huh?"

"A little," Lucy told her. "I love that you love me so much. And I love you that much, too. I just..."

"I know, sweetie. Your dad had a word or two to say about it before he finally went to bed. And I'm sorry, too. Now, what happened with Gavin and how is he?"

Lucy told her mother about the high fever spike, and the doctor's ultimate diagnosis, but then added, "Did you know that Gavin was only two pounds when he was born? And that he spent months in the hospital?"

Elaina nodded. "We had a prayer circle going at church. And made quilts for the babies, too," she said.

"When Gavin's fever spiked with no obvious sign of anything wrong, I think it took Noah back to those days. He called me to find out if Gavin had been out of sorts at Little Cowpokes that day. And he clearly needed a friend," she said. And then dared to add, "And I want to be that friend."

Not girlfriend. Not wife. But Lucy's needing to be the

one who answered when Noah called was pretty clearly out there, just the same.

And the mother-daughter relationship had survived.

Noah was still in the shower when the baby monitor mounted on the wall above the spray sounded. "No, no, no, no, no." Very clearly.

Charlie.

Had to be talking to Henry since Gav couldn't get out of the portable crib in the living room. Rinsing in seconds, he shut off the water with his face only half shaved. Grabbed a towel, and, dripping water as he went, he headed straight to the nursery.

The boys were safe, he told himself. Their toddler beds had bars high enough to keep them contained. But Charlie's words were definite indication of the need for a check-in.

Bursting into the room, Noah took in the scene in an instant. And stopped. Henry was still asleep, his knees underneath his belly, his butt up in the air.

And Charlie...the little man was standing in his crib, pointing to Gavin's empty bed. He turned when he heard Noah come in, and then immediately pointed again, shaking his whole arm toward Gav's bed in the process. "No. No. No. No. No," he said. He glanced back at Noah one more time and then to Gavin's bed again.

Tucking his towel in at his waist, Noah was at Charlie's side, lifting him out of his bed rather than taking the time to put down the bars as was routine. Charlie first, then Henry, then Gavin. Routine. But not right then.

"I know, son, it's okay," Noah said and, with the toddler's legs wrapped around him, whisked Charlie out of the room before he woke up Henry. He took him to the top of the stairs, where the living room was in full view below. "See," he said softly. "Gavin had a boo-boo and slept in his special bed."

Charlie nodded. Then stuck his finger in Noah's ear as he said, "Me spesh bed."

"You don't need your special bed right now, but Daddy needs to finish shaving. You want to help?"

When Charlie nodded, Noah handed the portable receiver for the baby monitor he'd set up in the living room to his oldest son and said, "Your job is to hold that and listen. If you hear Gavin, you tell me, okay?"

Taking the receiver in both hands, Charlie nodded, and as Noah made a beeline for the bathroom, the little boy dropped down to sit in the middle of the bathroom floor and stared at the thing as though his life depended on it.

Being responsible. Taking care of his little brother. At two.

Choking up with pride, Noah had only completed one swipe of his face when Charlie tossed the receiver aside, stood and grabbed at Noah's towel, pulling on it. "Me help," he demanded.

The towel dropped to a heap around Noah's feet. His son started knocking his fist against Noah's bare thigh. "Me help!" And Noah's phone sounded a text.

He glanced at the device he'd left on the bathroom counter and saw Lucy's text pop up.

Just saw this. Battery was dead. So relieved. Keep me posted. I'll be back over right after work, if that's okay.

Standing there naked, with Charlie pounding on his hip, Noah texted back, We'll be waiting. At the sounds of Henry waking up down the hall, he had to force the grin off his face so he could finish shaving without cutting himself.

Chapter Thirteen

Noah texted Lucy several times on Thursday while she was at work, missing the boys horribly. He'd let her know his mother and Cassie were at his house with the triplets while he worked, and were keeping in touch with him. All was well, but still feeling anxious, he'd ended his workday midafternoon.

Gavin's fever had come down, and other than being a little more clingy than usual, and pulling at his ear, he was back to his normal self. None of the grouchiness the doctor had warned him to expect.

He ate a good breakfast and lunch. As did the other two.

All three boys were asking for her. See MeWoo, Wooo Wooo, ooo ooo was the actual message he sent on that one

With every text, Lucy fell more in love. With Noah. And his boys. And hated, more and more, that she wasn't at Stargazer Ranch with those boys. Over the weeks Henry, Gavin and Charlie had been at Little Cowpokes, she'd taken on ownership—in a motherly sense. Ownership of the responsibility for their care.

With Gavin not feeling his best, her place should be with him.

Noah's afternoon text added that his mother had made a pot of barbecued pork and was leaving some at his place for dinner. As soon as she was able to leave the daycare that afternoon, Lucy drove to Tenacity Grocery for buns, stopped at a local stand to buy some freshly grown sweet corn, and then drove straight to the Stargazer.

Passing underneath the ranch's sign, she still felt like a stranger to the place, to the people who lived there, but as she pulled up to Noah's house on his spread, the sense of belonging that passed through her reinforced her feeling that she was right where she needed to be.

He was standing on the front porch, Gavin in his arms, when she got out of her car. Setting her bags down on the porch floor, she reached for Gavin, while Noah picked up her things and followed her inside.

Charlie and Henry threw themselves at her legs, both hugging her, and Lucy was grinning big as she saw Noah head with the groceries to the kitchen. As though she'd come home from work to his place innumerable times before. Like they were a team. In sync.

A feeling that continued to grow with her the rest of that week and through the weekend. When she wasn't occupied with a responsibility of her own, she was at the ranch. Watching the boys while Noah was out on the ranch. Helping in the barn. Even feeding Lewis and Jerry.

She was learning ranch life, Noah's life, and absorbing every minute of it as though it was the best food she'd ever tasted. As far as food for life was concerned, it *was* the best.

And every step of the way, Noah was there. Texting while he was out on the spread, or showing her what and how to do things when they were in the barn together. Usually with the boys running around them, making her lessons more like bits and pieces of things she'd fully grasp in time.

They didn't have sex. Or cuddle on the couch after the boys were asleep. Noah didn't even act as though he wanted to do so. But both Thursday and Friday nights, before she left to drive home, he held her, hands on her arms, and kissed her.

Deliciously.

Albeit with bodies held apart.

And both nights, he told her how glad he was that she'd come into their lives. Before asking her to drive safely and text him when she got home.

Which, of course she did. After which followed another half hour of back-and-forth musings about the day.

Ending with a Sleep well, see you tomorrow from him.

Getting up Saturday morning, knowing that she had a whole day at the ranch in front of her, Lucy felt as though she was glowing so brightly everyone would be able to see that light aura Winona had mentioned detecting around Lucy. Completing the chores she'd taken on at the house to help out her parents while she stayed with them, she showered and was on her way by the time the boys would be waking up.

She wanted the whole day with them. From breakfast to bedtime.

And by the time their bedtime arrived, Lucy was more energized than tired. She'd played games with the boys. Read through their entire bookshelf of books, having each one point out different things to her. Switching who got to sit on her lap with each book. Noah came in for lunch, and when he left again, without doing cleanup, her heart filled up some more.

Life wasn't just about the fun stuff. It was all the things. And one by one, Noah was sharing them with her. Allowing her to take up real space in their lives.

And that night, he insisted that she come upstairs with him to be a part of the triplets' bedtime ritual. The boys, lined up in the bathroom, standing by their impressively homemade potties, were stripped, encouraged to pee, washed, and then dressed in their overnight diapers and summer jammies.

"We brush teeth in the mornings, for now," Noah said, "but now that their molars are coming in, we're going to have to add a nightly brush as well." Lucy watched, learned, jumped in where she was a help not a hindrance—like when Gavin actually went quite a bit in his potty and she grabbed the bowl before Henry got to it.

The best part, though, was right before the three Trent warriors climbed into their toddler beds. Charlie grabbed a book, handed it to Lucy and then laid down on the floor, with the other two following suit, a space in between Charlie and the younger two. Noah, looking surprised, pointed her to the space. With her heart flooding, and her throat tight, she laid down in the middle of the floor, with all three boys on either side of her, their elbows on the floor, chins in their hands.

"Your turn to read, apparently?" Noah said, his voice

thick as he smiled at her. And there she was, in jean shorts and a T-shirt, lying on the carpet on the other side of Gavin and Henry, with Noah on the other side of Charlie as she read the short good-night book.

For a second, lying there, Lucy had a flashback to a night out in Denver. Dressed to the nines, going to a club with some friends, and then on to a concert to hear one of her favorite artists. She'd had a good time. And hadn't felt even half of the anticipation that was pumping through her as she lay on a nursery floor.

Happiness came where it came. And apparently landed even when one wasn't out looking for it.

She felt like one of the luckiest women on earth.

And she knew that life was giving her the moments that would remain as cherished memories for as long as she lived.

Noah wasn't ready for Lucy to go. But knew she couldn't stay. Not for long. Another night alone together, watching a movie, or having a beer and chatting was just too much of a risk.

Over the past few days, as he let himself open the door more and more to Lucy being a part of their lives, her presence in his home hadn't been the only thing that had increased.

Every time he'd walked in the door to see her there, tending to his home, his little men, or saw her in his kitchen, tending to the simple daily chores, his attraction to her had magnified.

He was a virile, healthy man who'd been without for a very long time. There was only so much stimulation he could take.

And they were still in the stage where everything seemed great. At their best. Excitement put people in good moods. The newness hadn't yet worn off, allowing everyday tension and frustration to set in. They hadn't seen each other at their worst.

Until they did, they wouldn't know whether that bill in the envelope was worth a buck or a million of them. And if it turned out to be a buck—and they'd already added a sexual component to the relationship—moving forward apart would be that much more difficult.

He'd been there, done that. Didn't see himself as ready to get through it again. And more, he couldn't stand the thought of putting another woman through it a second time. There were already people in town who thought he must have been pretty awful to live with to make a woman feel as though she'd rather leave her children behind than live with him.

He'd rather people thought that than to ever have his sons hear that their mother hadn't been able to handle the chaos of raising the three of them.

In a town like Tenacity there was no such thing as a private failure. People would always talk.

And with so many thinking he was already wrong to be saddling Lucy with his broken life and mammoth responsibilities...there was a chance they weren't wrong.

To get in that deep with Lucy and then fail her wasn't an option.

His pit stop done, and the beers he'd collected in hand, he found Lucy in a spotless living room, stacking the last of the toys in the trunk where they were stored. Instead of being out doing what she'd have been doing if he hadn't come into her life.

And it occurred to him…she'd entered his life. Had been inside the home where he grew up. Knew his entire life story and where everything went in his kitchen. While her life was still much of a mystery to him.

Much like Joanna's had been?

As he sat down, handing her a beer and holding his out to it, his toast came out of thoughts he hadn't meant to share. "Here's to the time when you share your life with me," he said.

Lucy clinked. Blinked. Raised her brows and said, "I'm sharing every free minute of my life with you."

At which he shook his head. Took a long swig from the one bottle he was going to get that night. And then said, "You're sharing your time with us. But you don't ever talk about you."

With a grimace, she said, "Did you ever stop to think that maybe that's because I don't have much of a life?"

He could only stare at that. Hard. Straight at her.

"I grew up. Went to college, where I dated five or six different guys in four years, none that I even came close to falling in love with. I didn't join a sorority because I had neither the money nor the time as I was working to help offset my expenses. I majored in marketing, graduated with straight A's. Interviewed for three jobs. Was offered all three. Took the one I most wanted. And when they offered me a lovely promotion and I wasn't excited at the thought of that being the next move in my future, I quit and moved home."

Facts in a nutshell. The kind of stuff he'd known about Joanna.

Joanna. It kept coming back to her. His failure. The blight on his life that he couldn't fix. For any of them.

Lucy sat back, crossing one long, slender, perfectly shaped thigh over the other.

Noah took another long sip to hide that he was drooling over her. Pulled at his T-shirt, making certain it was covering certain parts.

And he knew what he had to ask. What he and Joanna had never talked about. "Were you happy growing up?"

Lucy's smile seemed to suck the tension right out of him. "For the most part," she said. "As you already know, I'm super close with my parents," she started in. Frowned a little as she seemed to be looking inward and said, "I wasn't so sure about Tenacity growing up," she said then.

A statement that made her life the complete antithesis of his. He wouldn't let himself react. Had to sit without any kind of judgment and hear what she said. Listen to who she was.

"I think now it was more a product of being an only child. I was lonely a lot. And in Tenacity, there aren't a lot of families with onlys. Every year I'd go with my parents to the Fourth of July fireworks and all these kids would be playing with each other, and there I was, standing alone. No siblings. Just me and parents who wouldn't let me run willy-nilly through the park while there was 'fire in the sky.'"

At the way she said the last—her intonation—so obviously a quote, he smiled. And said, "I'll probably feel the same way about the tribe upstairs."

He was surprised when Lucy shook her head. "No, you won't," she said. "You're just the right amount of protection and chill. You teach. You watch out. But you let them fall where appropriate, too," she told him. "My mom, she worried about everything. She took me to the Quilting Club even though I was the only kid there. Always sitting by her side. I can't remember ever having a babysitter."

She'd been overprotected. Had had to leave town to get away from it. Lucy kept talking. Giving other examples. The way she complied, but also found a way to be herself. Like learning a love of crafts, but not a love of quilting.

He sat back, watching her, fascinated at the picture that was presenting itself. The formation of Lucy.

It was eye-opening.

And intoxicating, too.

"There was no way I was ever going to be able to find my own independence living under that roof, so as soon as I graduated high school, I hightailed it out of town," she said after a few sips of beer during a minute or two of silence. "I expected to find all the companionship, activities, opportunities and choices that would assuage the loneliness, and serve my need to assert my own independence. To make certain that my life was composed of my choices."

While there were nudges of returning tension, Noah was too engrossed to give them any heed. He was too busy admiring the ten-years-his-junior woman who seemed so much wiser than he'd ever been. He'd never considered where his life choices had been born. He'd just known they fit him and stayed within their boundaries as he'd branched out and found his own way.

"I realized, though, that it wasn't the town that had been the problem. To the contrary, thinking of Tenacity made me less lonely while I was away. I'd been running from a home that was ordered to the point of labeled shelves. And while filled with love, lacked...personality. I wouldn't say I was bored growing up as I did...but maybe..." Her voice trailed off and she looked at Noah, a faraway smile on her face. "Makes me sound kind of spoiled and pathetic, huh?" she asked.

There was so much Noah could say. But didn't. Holding back much of what he'd been thinking about her. The way he'd been reacting to her on and off for days on end. Needing to take her to his bed and talk in the age-old way of man and woman.

Instead, he just shook his head. Said, "No," and lifted his bottle to his mouth.

To keep his lips from reaching for hers.

The good-night kiss was getting close. Lucy could feel it coming on. Noah's withdrawal, while not physically evident, had become apparent to her over the past weeks. He was open. And then he wasn't. But, while in the beginning she'd worried that his withdrawal was due to him not being sure he wanted to be with her, now she was fully confident that was no longer the case.

He'd not only opened his home to her, exposing their relationship to his family in action if not in words, but he'd given her all access to his boys.

Insisting that she share bedtime had been the opening of the final door.

And as elated as she was with the way life was unfolding, she was dying, too. From lack of... Noah. Until they made love, they weren't lovers. They were friends.

She wanted that. Needed it. The friend part.

But she needed so much more. And, as the life story

he'd just pulled out of her had reminded her, the only way she was going to have a chance of finding her true happiness was to reach for it.

The rationalization was all there. Truth.

The heat about ready to spill out of her pores was what propelled her to set down her beer, lean over to take his and set it on the table beside him, and then, with a hand going straight to the hardness he'd been keeping covered with his shirt, she kissed him.

A real one. Like they'd had in the kitchen too long ago. Her mouth opened, her tongue teased his lips… and his lips didn't open. His hips lifting against her hand—she'd thought pushing into her—were…pushing her away?

It was the only conclusion she could draw as he pulled them back further into the couch than they'd been—putting distance between her grip and his pants.

And Lucy crashed. Hard. With the force of all the happiness she'd been soaking in over the past weeks pouring out to drown her in its shadow. Sorrow.

"I'm sorry," she said, standing. Looking around desperately. For something. Her purse. Where had she left her bag? She hadn't carried it in. She'd had Gavin. Noah had carried her bag. "Where's my purse?"

And her phone. She grabbed it off the coffee table, shoving it into her back pocket.

"It's in the kitchen," Noah said, leaning forward, his elbows on his knees. "What's going on?"

"It's pretty clear that you like having me around… as a friend…but I need more from you Noah. If I didn't feel about you like I do, I'd be fine with what we've got going on here. But I can't do this...wanting you when you aren't into...us...that way."

The last was said with her back to him as she headed to the kitchen. Remembering where her purse was on the way. She'd accessed it a couple of times that day. Hanging on a hook just outside the mudroom.

She'd thought he'd given it a permanent space in his home.

Choking back a dry sob as she snatched the straps from the hook and threw them over her shoulder, Lucy considered going out the back door and walking around the house to the front where her car was parked. After the embarrassing fool she'd made of herself, she figured it was better that she trek in the dark than walk back through the living room in front of him to the door.

She had the knob in hand when Noah's voice came out of the near darkness of the kitchen, not more than a foot or two away. "Where are you going?"

"Home."

"Probably a good idea," he agreed, his tone not translating into anything she recognized. "But not through the back door. And not until you give me a chance to respond to your accusations in there."

She hadn't accused anyone but herself. Had she?

Turning toward the sound of his voice, she made herself look at him in the shadows. His brow was furrowed. And he was closer than she'd thought.

"You accused me of not 'being into us' *that* way."

Not accusation. More like obvious assumption. The words came to her. She stood with them. Better that than let him hear the tremble she knew would be in her voice if she spoke.

"It's just not true, Luce. You're pretty much all I can think about these days. Right up there next to the boys. Before the ranch. Before anything else. And not just sexually. Though I've been hard more in the past two weeks than I've been since puberty. And let me tell you, it's not a pleasant thing to ride a horse with that suddenly going on."

A half sob, half chuckle spilled out of her. She wanted so badly to believe him. But… "Then why are you still holding back?" The question was little more than a whisper as he stepped closer to her.

Noah shook his head, his eyes gazing down into hers with a brightness she couldn't miss, even in the kitchen's near darkness. "Right now, I have no idea," he said, in a voice more low and gravelly than she'd heard.

His head lowered. She lifted hers.

And this time, when they kissed in the kitchen, neither of them pulled back.

Chapter Fourteen

With his lips still on hers, Noah slid an arm beneath Lucy's legs and lifted her petite frame up against his chest. Taking her back to the living room, he laid her on the couch, and then watching her, with her watching him, took the bottom hem of his shirt in his hands and slid it up over his head, tossing the T-shirt to the floor behind him.

She was staring at his chest, her gaze growing more smoky by the second. And when she licked her lips, he almost laughed with the pleasure surging through him. She was that turned on by his upper muscles, he couldn't wait to share the good stuff with her.

He grew more as he had the thought, and then lost all rational cognizance as Lucy met him move for move. Lifting her T-shirt up and over her head. Taking her bra with it.

A sport kind. No clasps. He'd sort of noticed. From a distance.

The rest of him was hearing the blood roaring through his veins as her beautifully shaped breasts stared up at him. Petite, like she was, they were bold like her, too. Protruding up at him. Nipples hard.

Noah dropped to his knees. Bent over her, and took one of those nipples into his mouth. Then his lips claimed hers again. Meeting her tongue for tongue. Hungrily. Unable to slow himself down.

With her help, they had her shorts down while he was still kissing her. And with only a couple of seconds-long breaks from their kiss, he got his wallet out of his jeans, secured the condom, dropped the rest to the floor, by which time she had his fly undone.

Noah had never shed a pair of jeans so fast in his life. One leg then the other, stepping on the bottom of one leg with his free foot as he pulled out, returning the favor on the other side. And then, kissing her once again, he climbed on top of her on the couch, reached down to find her deliciously ready for him, and slid himself home.

He nearly cried out with the almost instant release. Made more spectacular by the muscles contracting around him with her own satiation.

When it was through, he kissed her again. But needed air. With his head falling just over her shoulder, he gasped. Took in a deep breath. And then another.

Reality returned. Suffusing him with an entirely different kind of panic.

What in the hell had he done?

Rutting on her like an animal.

Lucy's chest started to pulse against him. In a rhythm he recognized. Sobs.

Pulling himself up to outstretched arms with his hands braced on the cushion on both sides of her, he had no thoughts other than that he had to fix things. Immediately.

He glanced down at her face, to see that she wasn't crying at all. The woman was laughing.

At him? He was so relieved that he hadn't made her cry, Noah didn't have enough awareness to care that she found sex with him laughable.

Reaching up to outline his lips with her finger, Lucy was looking at him with eyes glowing, and said, "So there was that. At least we were on the same page. Now what do we do for an encore?"

What he did was fall back down on top of her.

And then start to chuckle.

He was in way over his head.

And didn't care.

Kissing Noah's neck as he lay on top of her, Lucy was filled with the energy flowing through her, around them, and said softly, "You wanna' try again, taking it a little slower this time?"

"Yes," Noah said against her, and then lifted up, exposing her gaze to that incredible cowboy chest again. Muscled. Hard. Nothing spare anywhere. Unless you counted the tight, rough hair that she longed to run her fingers through.

He sat up before she had a chance. "But it needs to be upstairs," he said then, grabbing up her clothes to hand them to her before picking up his own. "I didn't bring down the portable receiver for the nursery monitor. A permanent one is installed on the wall just above my bed. One way of course. Nursery to me, not vice versa."

She knew what he meant. And started to hum inside all over again. Had he just invited her to his bed? As in, to share it with him?

"Are you inviting me to spend the night?" She was way beyond coy. She needed to know what she needed to know.

With a saucy grin he said, "I am."

Standing up, she turned, tossed a foot behind her, almost touching her butt, and proceeded to climb the stairs completely naked. She knew where his room was. Had had a glimpse of it when they'd put the boys to bed.

And while Noah brought in the dogs and turned off the lights downstairs, Lucy took care of necessary business in his bathroom. Used her finger and his toothpaste to brush. Texted her mom to say she wouldn't be home. And, when her lover came into the room, she was sitting up, posed for him, on the sheets of the bed she'd so neatly turned down.

There was no sleeping in when one had triplet toddlers. Noah woke as he always did, an hour before the tribe was due to stir. His eyes weren't even opened before he felt the major life change with which he was greeting the day.

Lucy. He could hardly miss her presence with his arm thrown over her waist. For a second he lay there in a quandary. Sunday was a day off for her. Did she like to sleep in?

He supposed she could do so in his bed. He'd just have to keep the door closed and the little men downstairs. Pulling his arm carefully away, he got about an inch from her stomach when she turned, eyes wide-open, and looked at him. "Morning," she said with a satisfied grin on her face.

Melting all over again, he gave a "Morning," right

back at her. He felt compelled to lean toward her, to start the day like they'd ended the night before. Was willing to forego his shower for the privilege.

Lucy held up a hand, shaking her head. "In the first place, I hate to be crass but I need to pee. And brush. But beyond that, we have three kiddos who are going to be up soon and I'd like to be ready for them."

If it was possible for Noah to fall any deeper into Lucy, he'd just done so. "Can we at least shower together?" he said, with a leering tone, and every bit of the magnetism that had had women flirting with him since he was teenager.

Lucy was already at her pile of clothes, pulling on panties he hadn't really even seen. They'd come off last night in a clump with her shorts. They didn't appear to be trendy. Or even sexy. Low-cut briefs that covered everything. Purple. He stood there hard, with no clothes to hide the fact.

"Better make that shower cold," Lucy chuckled as she pulled on her shirt. Sans bra. That went in her purse. He started to ache with the pressure of his need. While she headed toward the door. "I want to get home, showered, and back before they wake up," she said. "To see where I fit into the morning routine."

She froze in place as soon as she said the words. Looked over at him, eyes wide beneath a worry frown. "I'm sorry. I'm not meaning to push, or assume. It just felt..."

"Right," he finished for her, reaching her in a couple of strides. Taking her clothed hips in his hands. "And don't apologize for making us all happier, Luce." He leaned down and kissed her, then turned and got his butt beneath frigid water before he embarrassed himself.

Lucy had never been more in her element than she was that Sunday. She felt stronger, more confident than ever before. Ready to tackle whatever presented itself and come out okay. All five of them, seven counting Lewis and Jerry, spent a good part of the morning in the barn. Not just cleaning out stalls, but making a coop for chickens, too. Just for eggs for the ranch, not for profit. Something Noah had wanted to do since he'd first started his own spread. He was tired of getting eggs from his mother. And she was happy to relinquish that particular duty. He was buying the chickens from his parents. His insistence, not theirs.

And yet it made Lucy love him even more. Noah was a doer, not a taker. One who saw the lives around him and did what he could to bless them.

How the man could think himself selfish, she had no idea, but his stories about his breakup with Joanna always seemed to have that kind of vibe.

The little guys had a plethora of toddler tools, rakes, shovels. Even a miniature metal wheelbarrow that Charlie insisted he always had to push. They stayed surprisingly occupied in the area Noah had gated off for them to play in. Talking in gibberish to each other much of the time, and yet, responding as though they understood each other.

There'd been a screaming fit, too. Loud and ugly, with plenty of tears and snot involved, over a fight for a particular rake. And two minutes later, it was over. Faces

TARA TAYLOR QUINN   171

dry. And the brothers happily working together again. Getting whatever job they were doing done.

Late in the morning, Charlie was asking for a horsey ride, which turned out to be a bit harrowing for Lucy at first, as she watched Noah lift all three boys, one at a time, up onto a child-sized saddle on the back of Gazer, the smaller of his two horses. He stood right there by their sides, holding on to the back of their jeans, as he led them around.

She took a deep breath. And ended up getting videos of all three of them because their comfort and confidence in the saddle, as well as their joy, was so infectious. Just filled her with pleasure and pride, watching them.

Little-guy lunch was a loud and somewhat messy affair, and then, while Noah cleaned up, Lucy took the threesome upstairs for naptime. Reading to them while they each lay in their beds—exactly as she read to them as they each lay on their mats at Little Cowpokes. And before the book was half done, they were all three out. Even Charlie, who skipped naps anytime he could.

By the time she was back downstairs, Noah had grilled chicken wraps made for the two of them and took her out to the back porch, facing the mountain, to sit in matching rockers while they ate.

It was their first chance for any real conversation, and she had an item on the agenda. Taking a bite of sandwich, she cued up her phone and handed it to him, showing him the videos she'd taken. And then she watched the glow on his face as he watched them.

Him and his boys.

In their element.

The four Trent men, living in glory.

He watched them all twice, then said, "Send those to me," as he handed her phone back to her. Playing right into her agenda item. "Of course," she told him. And then, going with her heart's directions, she plodded right into an area that could be muddy. Or filled with sinking sand. But one that had to be traversed if they were ever going to collect their million-dollar bill.

"I think you should send them to Joanna," she told him. "You said she's working at a stable. With therapy horses. So this is an area where she can relate to them on her own terms."

Her stomach clenched over the couple of bites of sandwich she'd had. Until Noah turned his megawatt smile on her. "Great idea," he told her, as though she'd suggested apples instead of grapes for lunch.

Not like she'd just trespassed on private property, as she'd feared might happen. And that was when she knew that bill they'd talked about was most definitely a million. They'd made it through all the firsts. Had taken on a sick child together. And bath time that morning, too. Anytime she had a suggestion to make where the boys were concerned, Noah was appreciative as opposed to defensive. And the times he'd disagreed, he had reasons, based on experience she didn't yet have.

There'd be fights. Maybe even some loud ones considering how passionate they both were when they were together. But the pure happiness she felt sitting there—there was no doubt it was the real thing.

It was as though everything in her life had led her to that point. And because she'd been open to finding it, she'd recognized it immediately when a single father with triplets walked in the door and turned her on like none other before him.

And, thinking about their future, excited for all of the possibilities, she shared with him something her mother had told her that morning. "The woman I've been filling in for at Little Cowpokes is coming off maternity leave in the next week or two." She was leading up to other options, to discuss them with him. But stopped as his head swung in her direction. His mouth open. Eyes shadowed with concern.

"What are you going to do?" he asked. And then, his brow unfurling, said, "You can just come here. I'll pay you the tuition I'm paying the daycare."

The fact that his concern had been for her warmed her. The rest, not so much. "I don't need you to support me, Noah. I'm not looking for a sugar daddy."

As soon as she heard the words, she judged them to be too harsh. She wanted him to care. To have her back.

But... "I don't need you to fight my battles for me," she followed up as quickly as she could muster the words. "I'd love a lifetime of you fighting them with me, though."

As his face cleared, and he nodded, she continued, "I had no intention of giving up marketing. I like it to the point that other than deadline stress, it doesn't feel like work. I've been putting in applications ever since I got home. Had a phone interview, too." She was free-flowing at that point. She stopped and took a bite of sandwich. And swallowed before she glanced over at Noah.

He sat stiffly. His face expressionless. Staring up at the mountain in front of them.

And Lucy didn't need Winona's psychic skills to tell her that the temperature in their relationship had just suffered a cooling front.

"I'm not aware of any marketing positions in Tenacity," Noah said, taking great care to keep his tone conversational. With no hint of accusation.

Lucy had to follow her path. He needed that for her. And for him and his boys, too.

"I'm applying for remote positions," she told him, too quickly for his peace of mind. Trying to appease him? "I have no intention of leaving Tenacity. Remember, the little house I told you about? My plan was to make an offer as soon as I find the job I want. Living at home, working at the daycare, and with a bit of money saved, I can afford to take my time."

She wasn't planning to leave town. Good news. But how did you make such a plan when the key factor upon which everything lay was finding the right job?

"And if worst comes to worst, I can always take a job outside Tenacity and commute," she told him. "Bronco's only an hour and half from here, and there are probably closer opportunities, too."

The words were like a nail on a coffin he'd just started allowing himself to believe he wasn't going to need. How could she possibly make a promise without knowing a major part of her future? She'd never commuted before. Three hours a day spent traversing the same long boring road? Three hours wasted that she'd never get back.

Three hours plus a full day at work. To come home to three rambunctious little guys? Or not get home in time to see them before bedtime?

He could see the problems looming, even if she couldn't.

He was getting way ahead of himself. They'd had a few great weeks. And an incredible night in bed. They weren't even officially out as a couple yet.

But they'd gone into their relationship knowing that they both were looking toward a life, not just a season.

And right then a previous conversation they'd had hit Noah. A recent one. She'd told him that she'd quit her job and moved home because the promotion she'd been offered didn't excite her. That didn't mean another one wouldn't.

And if it did?

She wasn't currently planning on leaving town, but until she knew what was down her road, how could she possibly know that a life with him and his huge responsibilities was what she really wanted? She'd clearly thought the job in Bronco had been what she'd wanted. Time had shown her differently. His failing to recognize that point would be like Joanna all over again.

Because he felt in his heart that even if Lucy found the job of her dreams, with the caveat that she leave Tenacity, if she was with him, she'd turn it down. He could trust her to follow through on the commitments she'd make if they married, but down the road, if she couldn't pursue her own needs, she'd start to resent him. Or, if things got so bad she thought that the boys were suffering, she could leave…the way Joanna had.

He couldn't do it again. Couldn't reach for what was right for his life at the risk of someone else's not being what it was meant to be. Couldn't grasp his own future at the sake of another's.

Sitting there calmly, Noah simply froze inside. Froze out all of the great parts in the past several weeks.

Froze out hope.

He was thankful that he'd caught himself in time. Had seen the pattern. He'd forestalled a second tragedy. One that he sensed would have been far worse on him and the boys.

Noah didn't despair.

He also didn't finish his wrap. The lead in his stomach left no room for it.

Chapter Fifteen

Awash in despair, drowning with seemingly no ability to get to shore, Lucy clutched desperately for anything that made sense. A way out of water she hadn't known she was entering.

"Up! Up!" It almost seemed like fate when Charlie's voice came over the portable receiver Noah had brought outside with them. Time with the boys, where life came down to the simple truths that mattered most, seemed like certain rescue.

She and Noah could reconvene after the boys went to bed. They'd talk. Work things out. Standing with him, she started to follow him inside when he turned.

"I need some time, Luce," he said. His shortened use of her name was the only thing in that sentence that kept her upright.

Frowning, she hoped the rest of those words didn't convey a meaning as devastating as they'd sounded. "Time for what?"

"To think." He wasn't meeting her gaze.

He was very clearly blocking her entrance into his home.

"Up!" Charlie's demand was growing stronger. The littles had to come first.

She wasn't giving up on him. On them. And had no choice in that moment but to say, "I need my purse."

She waited outside while he got it for her. Needing his arms around her so badly she was shaking. But she didn't reach for him when he returned. Not even by look. "Will I be seeing you all at Little Cowpokes tomorrow?" she asked.

His confused frown, as though he was surprised there was any question, eased her heart a little. "Of course," he told her, hurrying back inside as Henry's voice added to Charlie's.

Lucy took slow deep breaths, and her time, on the drive back into town. Hanging her future on that *of course.* Taking all the strength she could from it.

She also tried telling herself that as she'd only known Noah and his sons for weeks, she'd be able to get over them if she had to.

But she didn't believe a word of it.

And wasn't going to stoop to lying to herself.

Which meant she had to face the fact that whatever it was that she'd said wrong, hadn't really been wrong. It was more likely that Noah was just getting cold feet. Living in fear from his past. What he'd gone through with Joanna wasn't going to go away just because he fell in love again. Most particularly not then.

If she'd thought hard enough, tuned into him more, she'd have realized that setbacks were a part of life. A given. Most particularly after something as emotionally encompassing, as incredible, as the night they'd just shared. He was afraid.

He'd made that clear from the beginning.

And he also was strong, responsible, determined. A

man like that didn't throw love away. Not for himself. And more particularly not for his boys.

By the time she pulled into her parents' driveway, Lucy was pretty much okay. Rationality, logical thought, leading to the hope that had drawn her and Noah together from the start.

Believing in the love she felt for him.

Drawing in a breath, she stepped into the kitchen and faced her mom. Asked what was for dinner, as though she'd planned all along to be home in time to eat it.

"Party casserole, your favorite," Elaina said, her tone easy, but her gaze filled with concern, and with the deep and abiding love Lucy's mother had wrapped her in from birth.

A security that set her free.

The same type of love she felt for Charlie, Henry and Gavin. Whom she'd be seeing in the morning. She needed new beads. Ones that looked like Gazer.

With a solid plan of action, she went to her room and pulled out the sculpting clay she was going to need.

But before getting started, she texted Noah, sending him the videos he'd asked for. Ones she trusted he'd send on to Joanna. He'd thought the idea a good one.

It took three texts. One for each video.

The first two bore no message. No words from her at all. Just the videos.

Almost as quickly as she sent them, he sent back two identical, simple Thanks.

On the third video, she drew on her belief in true love and said, Thank you for a wonderful weekend. I'm not leaving Tenacity, Noah. This is only the beginning.

And an hour later, she took his See you in the morning as a major win.

* * *

Noah fell into bed exhausted Sunday night. All three of his little guys had been cranky most of the afternoon and evening. He'd checked all for fevers. Looked in all ears for any sign of redness. Other than Gavin's left ear, the other five were fine.

Theirs hadn't been a sick kind of whiny. More like petulant. Overstimulated. They'd all had good appetites at dinner. Just hadn't wanted what he'd fed them. They'd wanted macaroni and cheese. Period. He'd discovered that after preparing and offering three other favorites only to have them shake their heads. Charlie gave emphatic *no*s. All three of them smeared cut-up banana pieces all over their trays, and then onto the floor. Along with the cut-up chicken he'd served with them.

After the macaroni win, though, they'd continued to be hard to please. Fighting with each other. Whatever toy one happened to pick up, another wanted.

There seemed to be only one thing they'd agreed upon. *MeWoo. Woooo. Oooo oooo.*

Noah felt them. Clear to his bones. *Lucy. Lucy. Lucy.*

She was gone by his choice, and her absence was eating at him. The boys had just woken to find her gone. He'd made an error in fatherly judgment. There'd been no goodbye for them.

And she'd very quickly become a part of their home. Gavin's illness, them needing her, her response…it had all been so natural.

So right.

Closing his eyes, he lay on his back, one hand on his forehead. Took a deep breath. And sat up.

He had to change the sheets.

Her scent, their scent, was all over them.

Up and at it, he had the chore done in minutes. Turned the light back off. Lay down.

She was still there. In his senses. In his mind.

And, God help him, in his heart.

Thank you for a wonderful weekend. I'm not leaving Tenacity, Noah. This is only the beginning. Her last text splayed across his mind behind closed lids. With nothing left with which to distract himself, he let it. Watched it scroll like a ticker tape. Over and over. Felt the relaxing of his muscles acutely as tension drained out of him.

He was as excited as his little men were as they headed into Little Cowpokes the next morning. In complete contrast to the bad moods of the night before, all three had woken up cheerful. Raring to go. The drive in had been accompanied by a series of "Mewoo," "Wooo," and "Oooo." In anticipatory tones, not tearful ones.

If they'd been older, they might have been hitting him over the head with their version of Lucy in their lives. He had no choice but to take heed. For their sakes.

But to do so cautiously. Teaching them that not everything lasted forever. That some people came and went. As they would one day go their own ways.

Hopefully at the Stargazer, but if not, he'd encourage and love them just the same.

How was he supposed to teach two-year-olds that lesson when he had no idea how to learn it himself? He hadn't yet figured it out. But he would. They had to count on him. He was all they had. The only one responsible for their care, he amended the thought as, heart rate a bit elevated, he strolled his crew into Little Cowpokes.

Hoping that Lucy's beautiful smile greeted them. That

he hadn't done irreparable damage the day before. But then, when the moment came, he didn't let himself look at her. He tended to his sons.

"MeWoo!" Charlie scrambled up as though his seat was on fire as soon as Noah had his straps released. Henry bucked up and down against his own straps, making it more difficult for Noah to provide the release the little guy was clearly after. When Gavin started in, Noah was about to let go with a firm command to all three of them, but then Lucy was there, unhooking Gavin's straps. He looked over at her. Right smack-dab into her waiting gaze.

"Having a tough morning?" she asked, grinning. Her knowing smile spoke to him so strongly that he didn't care if she was fully aware of his possible idiocy or not. She was there. With Charlie and Henry pulling at the hem of her denim shorts, and Gavin on her hip, his arm wrapped around her neck.

If it were possible to be jealous of his two-year-old son, Noah might have felt a twinge in that moment. Mostly, he couldn't completely wipe the smile from his face as he gave her an eye roll, and said, "I guess we missed you?"

With a quirk of her lips she said, "Seems that way." Just that, nothing more.

He needed more.

The boys knew their routine. They were pulling at her. Almost as though they wanted her to themselves. Or, at the very least, didn't want to share her with Noah.

Who was to blame for their lack of her the night before.

"You free to come by after work tonight?" he blurted,

even as he knew that there was no possibility that the toddlers could know that Noah had sent Lucy away.

Lucy's smile faded, and with it, Noah's burgeoning grasp at happiness. "Always," she said, her tone as serious as he'd ever heard it.

She turned her back on him then. As did his boys.

He stood there watching the four of them go. Filled with emotions he hardly recognized. Good ones.

The best ones.

He felt like a newly wealthy man as he drove back to his spread, donned his cowboy hat and spent the day working his butt off.

For his family.

Turned out to be quite the eventful day. Not only had Noah invited her back in, Lucy heard, officially, that she would no longer be needed at Little Cowpokes by the end of the week.

And the Denver offer came in. She was checking her email during her quiet after-lunch lunch in the deserted reception area, saw the address and tried not to get her hopes up as she clicked to open. Heart pounding, she let out a small squeal, and then read on. She was taken aback by the value the company saw in her. As proven by dual offers, and more money than the job had posted for.

They'd put her brand of marketing—find the customers who need a particular product, who fit it, rather than convincing someone who had no use for it to try it—out to some key clients and the response had been overwhelming.

While she was rereading the email for the third time, taking it all in, Noah texted. He'd run into some trouble with one of his herds. Said that his mother would be coming in to pick up the boys, but that he hoped she'd still make it out after work.

A most definite sign that he'd worked through the fear engrained by his traumatic experience with Joanna. Emboldened by the Denver offer, she texted back that she could borrow car seats from Little Cowpokes, and bring the boys home herself. Consciously and purposefully challenging him to give her that much of a place in their daily lives. And when he texted back, That would be great. See you in a few hours, she sat there grinning. Asking herself what was making her happier. Noah's reaching out for who and what they could be together? Or the incredible job offer? But she knew the answer before she asked.

Family with Noah. Hands down.

But the offer—most definitely her favorite icing on top of the cake.

She'd taken a risk, turning down the Bronco promotion. Moving home. The choice could make her appear as someone who wasn't committed to the career she'd chosen. A kiss of death in her field. But all of her soul-searching, her self-honesty, had led her home anyway. And in one day, everything was finally coming together.

Life's way of confirming that she'd made choices that were right for her personal journey.

With a full car—and an incredibly full heart—Lucy headed out to Stargazer Ranch later that afternoon, glancing into her rearview mirror as often as it was safe to do so. Pinching herself, almost literally, to believe that she had three kiddos that she loved, belting

out their renditions of the song she'd put on for them.
As she sang along with them.

It was a tune they played often at Little Cowpokes and
Charlie had almost all of the words down. His rendition
of them, anyway. Most of which were identifiable to her.

As soon as she'd known she would be driving them
home, she'd spent the rest of her lunch break download-
ing to her phone an entire playlist of songs that would
be familiar to them. Just in case any of the three were
stressed riding in unfamiliar car seats, or having her as
their driver for the first time.

She needn't have worried. Apparently, the same kind
of life forces that Lucy relied upon had guided her three
passengers to trust her. Or, at the very least, they could
feel her love and wanted more of it.

Which worked out just fine as she had an unending
well of it to share with them. And proceeded to do so
for the rest of the day and into the evening. They played.
After a text from Noah, they went with Lewis and Jerry
to feed the horses. The boys ate. And were in their jammies, ready to lie down and listen to story time when
Noah, his herd situation finally under control, made it
back to them.

The joyful squeals and hugs that flew at him as he
appeared in the doorway to the nursery brought tears to
Lucy's eyes. For the boys' sakes she blinked them back.
They were too young to get the concept of happy tears.
But she didn't even try to hold back the swell of love
that had prompted them.

And she was still brimming with it when she and
Noah sat at the kitchen table half an hour later, eating
the chicken and green bean casserole he'd brought over

from the big house on his way home. Olive was such a great cook.

Lucy hoped to be as good someday. And said so as she and Noah were cleaning up. Dinner conversation had consisted of him telling her about the situation that had erupted that afternoon—a mountain lion, suspected to be rabid, had attacked a small herd. Noah had lost one bull. But had captured the mountain lion. Several other members of his herd had been injured, and had all been rounded up and tended to. All were being kept cloistered, waiting for the rabies test results, which were expected in the morning.

"You like to cook?" Noah asked behind her as he hung a kitchen towel and followed her into the family room.

She shrugged. "When I don't have something more pressing to do," she told him, grinning. "How about you?" They'd made it to the point of domesticated conversation. The day just kept getting better and better.

"Same," he told her, the look in his eye darkening as he sat down beside her. A most definite, silent communication regarding the sex that was about to be had.

Something she desperately wanted. But she had to tell him about her news, too. She'd be gone for a couple of weeks of training. She had been offered the chance to start immediately, or as soon as she was available, and needed to talk to Noah about when he thought it would be best for her to be gone, in terms of calls on his time and the boys' needs.

"I had a job offer today," she told him. "With my first choice company," she added. Turning on the couch to face him, she was excited to share the company's words about her. "I had to write in one paragraph my approach to and philosophy of marketing. I didn't know why at the time, but I found out the company put out all applicants' answers to their top clients and I was picked first by every one of them." She was smiling. Noah was too, and so she continued.

"The job is remote, exactly what I wanted, and they offered me more money than was posted if I was willing to take on multiple clients at a time. Which I did all the time in my last position." Suffused with all of the good happening around them, she went on to share, "They actually offered me a second opportunity, if I wanted it. An in-house managerial spot. At twice the money." She kind of chuckled at that one. It just felt so good to be so highly valued. To be wanted.

It took her a second to realize that Noah wasn't exuding any joy.

Which shocked her. He was so careful to make certain that her personal life was in the picture. That would include celebrating her victories, too.

She'd been thinking about a glass of wine, to toast the offer. But he wasn't celebrating. "What's wrong?" she asked, ready to take on whatever concern had surfaced and find a solution with him.

His smile came then. A genuine one. It reached his eyes. And seemed to be tinged in sadness, too. Covertly. But there. "Nothing!" His tone fit the assurance. "I'm really proud of you, Luce. And not at all surprised, either. We should have a glass of wine, to toast." He stood as he spoke, and was already halfway to the kitchen, his back to her, by the time he finished.

Relief flooding through her, Lucy waited, sitting in

the warmth of his home, hugging herself. The man was an enigma she was looking forward to deciphering for the rest of her life.

He came back in and handed her a glass. She raised it as he held his out, heard his "Congratulations!" But his odd tone drew her gaze to his and, without toasting, she put her glass down.

"What's wrong?" she asked again.

Sitting down next to her, he sipped alone. She stared at his glass as he set it down. Couldn't take her gaze away from that liquid.

He'd sipped alone.

"Nothing's wrong." His voice, soft and sweet, eased the sudden tension in her stomach some. Enough for her to turn and look at him. "Everything is happening as it should," he continued. "In a timing that can't be ignored."

She'd had the thought several times that day. So why did his rendition seem to carry something other than an eventual wedding ring? He was genuinely happy for her. She could see his pride for her in his expression. There just didn't seem to be anything beyond it.

Feeling as though she was standing on a bomb that could detonate if she moved at all, Lucy sat there. Waiting. Hardly breathing. Not even thinking. Just...waiting.

"You need to take that managerial position, Luce," he said then. "There's no way I'm going to hold you back."

Mouth open, she stared. She hadn't even considered the second offer. Had just been flattered by the fact that it existed.

"I want the remote position," she said, making certain that her choice was very clear. "I applied for it before you and I were even a thing."

"Did you know the second opportunity existed?" he asked then, as though it was critical that she understood the magnitude of what was on the table.

"No, but I wouldn't have applied for it had I known. I want a life in Tenacity, Noah. I told you that."

"You said you quit your job because the promotion didn't excite you. You came home to figure out what was next. Clearly, this is what's next for you. The excitement in your voice is unmistakable."

His tone was still warm. Encouraging.

Filled with love, even.

"It wasn't like that," she told him. "When I got that earlier offer and wasn't excited, I knew that I was heading in the wrong direction. I asked myself what *would* excite me. And the answer was there. As much as I liked my job, had a knack for it, and felt like I could make a difference with my brand of marketing, having a life in Tenacity, living in this town where I'm known and loved, where I know and love so many, being a part of keeping it alive, of raising a family here, was what excited me."

"Just because Bronco, and that one job, didn't do it for you, doesn't mean that there isn't more out there for you. You need to experience everything the world has to offer."

Taking what felt like her last shot, Lucy opened her heart completely and said, "You and the boys are my world."

A noticeably thick swallow was the only indication Noah gave that her words hit home with him. That they mattered. Still, hope hung there as he opened his mouth and took a breath. Right up until she heard the words that followed it.

"I can't just sit here and watch you settle, Luce." The words were like bullets to her heart. Noah wasn't even going to try?

To fight for her? For them? The family they could make together?

His next words killed her.

"And that's why you need to go."

Chapter Sixteen

Noah stood as Lucy did. He turned toward her, to wish her well—a must—only to watch her walk the long way around the table to avoid him. She grabbed her purse. And without a backward glance, let herself out the front door.

He was still standing there, frozen in place, when he heard her car start and pull away.

He thought about moving to the window. To watch her headlights as far as he'd be able to see them, until they disappeared around one of his father's barns in the distance.

Instead, he put his hands in his pockets and blinked the tears out of his eyes.

Then calmly picked up the glasses of wine. Poured the celebration down the drain, dropped the glasses in the dishwasher and headed upstairs.

He'd done the right thing. Checking in on his sons, he felt the conviction of having made the best choice for their future. As much as they'd missed one night with Lucy, they'd suffer a millionfold if she was with them for a few years, long enough for them to carry lifetime memories of her, and then left.

In bed, remembering Lucy there with him, he lay with

conviction in his heart. As much as she loved him and the boys, she had no idea what she was giving up. But she would wonder in the future, when life in Tenacity became mundane. When the reality of raising another woman's children started to matter to her.

When the boys grew up enough to be some part of Joanna's life.

The thought had him sitting up and turning on the light. It wasn't late enough for him to be in bed. He'd never sleep.

Pulling on his jeans, leaving the shirt, he walked barefoot downstairs and, portable receiver in hand, out through the mudroom, talking softly to his mangy mutts, calling them outside to sit with him on the stoop.

Looking out over what he could of his land in the darkness. Knowing that, in spite of how god-awful he ached inside, he'd done the right thing.

It was killing him to think of how badly he'd hurt Lucy. But he believed deep down that she'd be thankful later that he'd set her free.

As he had Joanna.

Thinking of how much happier and healthier his ex-wife was since he'd told her to go follow her heart, he pulled out his phone and called her.

They'd been friends for the majority of their lives. Something that hadn't changed since their divorce. Which became apparent to him when, a few sentences into their conversation, she said, "You sound down. What's going on?"

She asked in the same way she used to do. Before marriage and a family had messed them up. Her question was filled with compassion. And an ability to take on whatever he had to say.

TARA TAYLOR QUINN   193

She'd always cared. And his stuff no longer had any impact on her everyday life.

Because he trusted in both, he said, "I met someone."

"And?" As in, *What's wrong about that?*

"She's a career woman, Joanna. A talented one. I just told her to accept a great job opportunity that came to her."

"Of course you did. It was the right thing to do."

"I think I love her."

"Does she love you, too?"

"I think so."

"Enough?"

He shrugged. Realized she couldn't see him. But still didn't speak. He had no answer to the question. It was never enough if it meant one person giving up their life to live another's.

She, more than anyone, would get that. And on that thought, he asked, "How are you doing?"

"Great, actually." The response was tempered—in lieu of his recent outpouring, he was sure.

But he heard a happiness in her voice he didn't recognize. And said, "Tell me about it." Hearing Joanna's happiness lifted his spirits some. It was confirmation that painful times led to better days ahead.

"I've met someone, too," she told him, her tone odd enough on the "someone" that he had to ask, "Who?"

"My trainer, actually," she said. And then added, "The woman who's teaching me how to train horses for therapy work."

A woman.

It clicked. Completely. Joanna hadn't just been settling for the wrong type of life with him. But the wrong type of person. He'd never known. Hadn't even considered...

But he wasn't shocked, either.

"She's eager to meet the boys, and you know, Noah, with her around, I think I won't take so much on myself and blow things. Just for a short visit. When it's convenient, of course. But maybe...you know...at some point... we can do video calls and stuff? So that they know that even though I don't live with them, I do love them?"

Feeling as though life had come full circle, Noah smiled, kind of sadly, and when he said, "I'd like that, Joanna. Just say when," he meant every word.

"I hope you like her," his ex-wife said then, sounding more like the woman he'd lived with that last year or so of their marriage.

"I already do," he said, a genuine smile on his face. And couldn't forstall the next part, either. "She's good to you?" he asked.

"Yeah, and the best part, Noah, I'm good for her, too."

And that right there was the crux of it all. In every relationship. In his and Lucy's, she'd most definitely been fabulous for him and his tribe. But there was no way they were good for her. Not if he allowed them to hold her back.

Noah sat outside with his dogs for another hour after he hung up from Joanna.

Letting go.

And when he went into bed, he was able to sleep.

Lucy had come full circle. She was back in Bronco, with a promotion offer awaiting her response. And the desire for a life in Tenacity raising a family calling her home. Except that she wasn't in Bronco. She was in Tenacity, with the life she so desperately wanted not wanting her. And a lucrative job offer in Denver awaiting her response.

That afternoon, when the Denver offer had come in, she wouldn't have dreamed of leaving Tenacity. As she lay sleepless in bed Monday night, all cried out, getting away felt like a good idea.

She'd been so certain that her self-honesty, listening to her heart, trusting her instincts, would lead her to the life she was meant to live. To happiness and fulfillment. She and Noah would have faced challenges. She had no doubts about that. Life was hard sometimes.

Elaina had been completely right in the warnings she'd laid down ad nauseam when Lucy had first started seeing Noah. They were ten years apart in age. He'd be ready to retire when she was still a decade away from health care benefits. She was not the biological mother of his children. Another woman, Joanna, would always be a figure in their lives.

Those things should probably have bothered her. They just hadn't. The feelings between her and Noah, the connection she'd been certain they shared, had left no room for doubt. Lucy had seen a clear path where she and Noah were a team that would work together to help Joanna be as much a part of the triplets' lives as she could be. Lucy's heart welcomed Joanna. Hurt for the woman's struggles. There was just no threat there.

And if fates had shined upon them, she'd have had biological children of her own with Noah, too. He would have someone to share middle-of-the-night feedings. Or actually just do them, since she'd hoped to breastfeed.

Still, there'd have been problems. Noah was right, too. There were things that would have presented that they couldn't yet see. But that was always true. No matter who the person, or which path they chose.

There were bumps in every road. If you stayed on it long enough.

She'd seen it all, felt it all, so clearly. As though she'd had a direct line to fate, and just had to trust what she knew.

But what if she was the one who'd been wrong? Everyone else, her mother, Noah, even members of the Tenacity Quilting Club, had tried to warn her. They were all older than her. More experienced. Had they been right all along? And she, in her youth, had been too pigheaded to listen to them?

Noah had made the same mistake with Joanna, hadn't he? In a sense. His ex-wife hadn't actually talked to him about her innermost needs, but he'd been so filled with what he'd known his life course to be that he'd plowed forward, without any thought at all to Joanna's needs not fitting in. She'd loved being at Stargazer Ranch. Had preferred to hang out with Noah than anyone else. It had made sense for them to marry. And the marriage had turned out to be a tragic disaster.

Noah had been down that road. Had traveled the path. He had the experience. Knew all of the bumps in the road. And had been trying to tell her about them, to prevent them from falling down the same hellhole since the day they'd met.

Lucy had been the one pushing things. Insisting that she knew all. Knew better than everyone else.

Doubting herself, Lucy fell into a troubled sleep. And

woke up Tuesday morning with new resolve. To listen to others. To learn from them. To trust that she had a lot to learn, rather than thinking she knew it all. As soon as she was up and showered, she emailed her job acceptance.

She was waiting for Elaina when her mother came down for her first cup of coffee. The conversation was short, tearful and ended with a hug that Lucy guessed was going to sustain her for the rest of her life.

She had breakfast with her dad. Elaina had been keeping him filled in every step of the way, as always. He didn't have a lot to say. Just, "You've always had a wisdom about you, Lucy. If you think this is the right thing to do, then it is."

Unable to respond for the tears clogging her throat, hearing irony where he'd meant support, she nodded, hugged him, too. And by noon, she was in her car on the road to Denver. She'd only packed essentials for the couple of weeks of training. Would take the time to pack up her life again, to rent a trailer to haul everything, when her wounds had had a little time to heal.

The drive was long. She didn't get to Denver until after midnight. Following her car's on-board mapping system to the address of the hotel the company had given her, she pulled into the well-lit upscale hotel valet parking area, and suddenly had a view of herself as if from outside looking in. As others would see her. And she recognized that even as young as she was, she had a lot to offer. Had developed skills that others could use.

Executives from Washington Marketing Resources had rented the room—within walking distance of their corporate office—for her for a week, giving her time to find a place to live.

They were thrilled that she'd agreed to be a part of their team.

She met so many new people on Wednesday that her head was spinning. She felt a lift in her spirits, too. Saw possibility for happiness in her future. She was immediately ensconced in conversations and potential problem-solving that required full concentration. And a tapping into, and sharing of the unique skill set she'd developed during college and the years of work afterward.

Over the next couple of days, she felt energy returning. Couldn't wait to get to the office. Brought client files to study back to the hotel with her at night. The distraction was a godsend.

And while she had to constantly fight off the stabs to her heart that came with every thought of Henry, Gavin and Charlie—when lunchtime hit, quiet time, bath time, bedtime, pickup, drop-off, dinner, morning lineup for pee practice—she took on the battle. Would continue to wage it until she won. With Noah, she didn't even try. She was in love with him. Maybe she'd meet someone someday that grabbed her heart away from him, but she didn't think so.

The one thing she absolutely did not do, refused to allow, no matter the cost, was text Noah. He'd made it clear that he didn't trust her to know her own mind well enough to make the best decisions, long-term, for his sons. Maybe rightfully so. Though, even with days passing, she couldn't seem to shake the sense of rightness about the two of them together.

What she did know was that she needed a man who wanted her one hundred percent. One who would fight for them. For their relationship. In spite of what might be valid fears.

They could have found a way. She could have done the training in Denver. Taken the remote job. Bought her little house in town. And in time they could have married.

Instead, he'd turned his back on them.

On the exact day that Washington Marketing had offered her far more than she'd asked to have.

As she got ready for work the next morning, a new thought struck.

Maybe fate hadn't deserted her after all.

It felt good to be so valued. To be wanted and needed. To be enough, in spite of only having lived for twenty-four years.

The week that Lucy left Tenacity did not go well for Noah. Starting with Tuesday morning drop-off when Elaina Bernard, rather than Lucy Bernard, met him in the reception area to escort his little men to their playroom.

"Where's Lucy?" The question had come even before his three had started their renditions of calling for her.

"On her way to Denver," had been all the woman had told him. She'd been kind. Professional. And had left Noah with no sense whatsoever as to what she thought of the situation. Or him.

He'd have thought she'd be elated. That, at the very least, she'd be thanking him for saving her daughter from throwing away her life.

From that point on, Angela Corey had been the one to meet him for drop-off and pickup.

The triplets had been out of sorts all week. Charlie peed on the floor three out of the four mornings of potty training. Henry peed in the bathtub, requiring Noah to outboard all three, keep them contained while he disinfected the bathtub, and then load them all back in.

On Friday, when Noah pulled into Little Cowpokes, Charlie crossed his arms over the straps on his car seat, shook his head and said, "No. No no no no!" It took an extra five minutes to get his sons inside. Two of them were in tears as Angela led them off, with calm and kind assurances to Noah that they'd be fine.

When he'd called half an hour later, the daycare owner had put him on a short video call to show him that she'd been right. The boys were all engaged in a coloring project. None of them looked happy to him, but he knew from experience that they would be.

Children were far more resilient than adults. With them not quite two yet, the chances were that they'd forget Lucy with time.

Unlike their dad, who seemed destined to spend the rest of his life randomly reliving some of the best moments of his life. And sending out love and good thoughts to the incredible woman who'd given them to him.

Thankfully the rabies test had come back negative on the mountain lion, so his cattle were out of quarantine, and back on the range. But Noah was spending extra hours riding fence line. Protecting his cattle from future dangers that could befall them.

Which was where Ryder found him Friday, early in the afternoon. Also on horseback, Ryder reined in beside him.

"What's up?" Noah asked, though he figured he knew. It had only been a matter of time.

He'd been avoiding the family all week. Which was his prerogative. And a choice they were supposed to respect. They'd all had a lot of practice getting that one right after Joanna left.

"You, that's what," Ryder said, sending a glance that Noah chose to take through peripheral vision only. And that, only partially, as they both had their cowboy hats pulled low due to the late June penetrating sun.

"Let it go, Ry."

"Yeah, you'd think I would, wouldn't you?" Ryder said, keeping an even pace with Noah rather than trying to best his big brother and set the pace, hoping Gazer would follow his lead. "Turns out, not this time." Ryder's tone was...sincere. Oddly so. To the point that Noah did spare him a glance.

And then ignored the comment.

"I'm the one who loves 'em and leaves 'em, big brother." Ryder didn't take the hint and shut his damned trap. "With the women knowing the score going in," he added, with a cocky nod.

Noah continued to ride fence line. Checking the herd and the perimeters with focused eyes.

Ryder came at him again. "And you'd think that my lifestyle would have me patting you on the back right about now."

Noah bit back something along the lines of if his brother didn't shut up he'd be doing more than patting *him* on the back. More like a brotherly brawl to tape his mouth to shut him up.

"Just because I'm not into monogamy, the whole emotional commitment thing, doesn't mean that I don't recognize its value. You know, for those for whom it fits."

Movement a hundred yards ahead caught Noah's eye. He kept his attention on the spot as he slowly approached.

"You love her, man." Ryder's voice came from outside Noah's circle of concentration. An irritating sound, at best.

"You're a fool for letting a good woman like her get away. Just saying."

With an instant heel to Gazer's side, Noah pulled ahead of Ryder, cutting him off with Gazer's side to Ryder's mare's head. "Where do you get off trying to advise me on a love life? Coming from a guy who's never had one?" He bit out the words through gritted teeth.

Ryder's chin lifted, as though daring Noah to punch it. "Just answer me this," his little brother said, challenge in his tone. "You really being self-sacrificing here? Or just protecting that bruised heart of yours?"

The words depleted every ounce of Noah's anger. Falling back in line with Ryder, continuing his perusal of his spread, he eventually gave an honest answer.

"Both."

Chapter Seventeen

The last day of June, a Monday, was Lucy's turning point. She still hadn't looked at a single place to live. She was due to check out the next morning.

And instead, extended her stay another week, putting the bill on her own credit card. Maybe a week wasn't long enough for her to grow up, or know what she really wanted out of life.

Or maybe she'd known all along.

And had just let Noah's rejection make her doubt herself.

Thing was, she hadn't moved home to Tenacity for Noah. She'd been following her heart's desire for the type of life she wanted.

In the small hometown where she'd grown up. The town that filled the vacancies in her heart just by being there for her.

Presenting herself in her direct superior's office first thing that morning, she turned down the managerial position that was still on the table. And signed all of the paperwork required to take the remote position.

"You're sure?" Rebecca, vice-president of client satisfaction, asked, her doubts about the wisdom of Lucy's decision written all over her face.

And, standing in the doorway of the lush, private office—similar to one that could be hers someday—Lucy felt a genuine smile break out on her face. "The work I like most, what I'm best at and—more importantly—the work that energizes me is the creativity," she said. Filled with so much conviction she knew the words to be complete truth. Her current truth. Which was all anybody ever had. It wasn't like human beings could predict clear, complete visions of the future. "I get excited about bringing people to products that will bless their lives," she said then.

Rebecca looked shocked. And then, standing, she smiled in a way Lucy hadn't seen over the past week. Holding out her hand to Lucy, she said, "Then we're honored to have you as a client specialist on our remote team," the executive said. Adding, "Truly. Welcome to Washington Marketing Services as an official member of our team."

Another hour of meetings followed the paperwork. And as soon as she was back in the temporary workspace she'd been assigned for her training period, Lucy was on her phone, making flight reservations. The office was closed on Friday, for the Fourth of July. And the Fourth of July in Tenacity was one of those times the entire town came together to celebrate. She was going to be there.

Because Tenacity was her home. And where she belonged.

She'd made the right choice to leave Bronco. Had been right all along. Being a wife and mother was her first calling. The mistake would be to let heartache prevent her from reaching for her real dream. Raising her family as she'd been raised. In Tenacity.

Noah could keep her away from him, from those kiddos she was missing so much it hurt, but he was not going to rob her of the rest of her life.

Noah woke up Friday morning with a pit in place of his stomach. The boys had learned about the Fourth of July at Little Cowpokes that week. Mostly because the daycare, like all of the other businesses and clubs in town, had a float in the annual parade. Charlie, Henry and Gavin had special T-shirts they'd be wearing as they rode in the miniature hay wagon their grandpa had made specifically for the occasion. Independence Day was old-fashioned in Tenacity. The parade was followed by a picnic and then a party that continued until after dark, ending with fireworks in the park.

"Fire. Ky," Charlie had told him repeatedly since they'd seen pictures of what would happen.

Noah understood the toddlers' excitement, even if they didn't yet grasp anything beyond the fact that everyone around them was hyped up about the occasion. Since Noah was old enough to remember, the Fourth of July had seemed akin to Christmas in Tenacity. And there he was lying in bed, dreading the day.

The town had been decked out for the holiday in red, white and blue bunting for more than a week. Noah had taken it all in, with extra care, every time he'd driven into town for drop-off and pickup. He had carefully laundered the boy's new T-shirts after Angela gave them to him. Had even helped his father with the hay wagon, ensuring that the boys would be safe inside.

For extra measure, he'd be walking beside the thing through the entire parade, to ensure that none of his brood climbed out for some of the candy that would be tossed to passing participants and into the crowd.

With both sides of Central Avenue filled with school kids holding their buckets and bags as they watched with anticipation for flying goodies, racing to grab what they could before someone else got there, he could see any of his three trying to follow suit.

If he had his preference for the day, Noah wouldn't take them anywhere but out to his barn. To let them ride around on Gazer. Feed them candy that he bought for them since they weren't going to be able to scramble for any. To grill hamburgers and hot dogs, and pretend that they had all they needed right there.

But he couldn't deprive the boys.

One of his babies had expressed his heart's desire the night before. Noah had thought all three were asleep as he'd been standing in their room after story time. But Charlie had popped up to say, "MeWoo to Fork Hoowee," and then laid back down.

The boys didn't know that Lucy was no longer in town. Nor would they probably be able to grasp the concept at that point. To them, the entire universe was made of up Tenacity city limits and the Stargazer.

And even if they knew, how did he tell them that she was gone and it was all his fault? Every day, at least one of them called out for her when they got to Little Cowpokes.

A couple of nights before, when Noah had put Charlie in his high chair, he'd looked up with such a serious expression on his face and had said, "MeWoo, eat?"

Surely, at less than two, his little guys should have moved on after a couple of days, at most, right?

How in the hell could he expect them to accomplish something he was failing to succeed at himself?

But he would.

With that thought, Noah was out of bed, in the shower, shaved and dressed in record time. Even if Lucy had still been in town, and a part of the day's festivities, she was no longer a part of their lives.

Noah, in his sense of superiority due to his vast experience, had made certain of that.

He knew that he'd made the noble gesture for her as much as for himself and his young sons.

While at the moment he ached with every breath he took, in the future, he'd at least be able to live with himself.

Lucy was decked out in a short denim skirt, a red, white and blue tie-dyed flowing tank, and white wedge sandals on Friday morning. Standing on a portion of the curb on Central Avenue as she waited for the parade to start. With Rebecca having proclaimed that she'd exceeded training expectations and was free to go, Lucy had canceled her weekend flight home, and had driven in the day before. Arriving just in time to have a late dinner with her folks and drop into bed.

She had already made an offer, via email, on the little house she wanted. It wasn't big enough for the family she hoped to have one day, but when her life situation changed, she could rent the place out. Maybe put the income in a savings account for college funds for her children.

At the moment, the only children on her mind were Gavin, Henry and Charlie. Unless Noah boycotted the Fourth of July, she was going to be seeing the boys. Knowing that they were no longer hers to hug.

Elaina had warned her that Christopher Trent had made a special wagon for the triplets, as part of the Little Cowpokes parade display.

By the time the parade started past her she was shaking inside. Had her hands folded and up against her chest, as though she was shivering from cold, not nerves. Elaina had failed to tell her just where in the parade Little Cowpokes would be positioned. A friend from high school came up behind her, stopping just to say she was in town for the weekend. And that they should meet up at the Social Club the next night, and Lucy nodded. Grinning. Wanting to go.

She was home. Life was starting anew.

The floats passing by—mostly simple hay wagons dressed up with plywood, poster board and tissue paper, with a good bit of markers and paint thrown in—represented the neighborhood businesses and community organizations. She smiled and waved at people she knew as they passed. Watched kids scramble for the candies that riders on the floats tossed out to them. Remembering being one of those kids herself.

Remembering the fun she'd had as though it had been a month before instead of more than half her life ago.

And then she tensed again. The mobile grooming truck Git Along Little Doggy was moving slowly up the street, Noah's sister Renee behind the wheel, with her fiancé, Miles Parker, in the passenger seat. Both of them lived on the Stargazer. In a cottage that backed up to the same mountain as Noah's house. Renee honked just as she passed Lucy, which had her in a quandary that took some of her strength. Had Renee purposely honked to her?

Because she didn't disapprove of her and Noah together? Or as a sign of support?

Or just a random honk like the one she gave out a few dozen yards up the street.

The Tenacity Quilting Club float was next, festooned with red, white and blue crocheted garlands.

And Lucy smiled through the sudden tears in her eyes. Every single truck, car, walking crew and float that passed told something about the history of Tenacity. And Lucy knew every story.

That was what mattered to her. Living where she knew. And was known.

Caring not just for those who lived in her house, but for those who walked the same streets, shopped at the same stores, lived next door. She cared about their victories. Their hardships.

Tenacity was a poor city by comparative wealth standards, but it had more to offer Lucy than any amount of money ever could.

The grand marshal's float was next, a flatbed wagon with a bench tied to the front wall, bearing a lavishly decked-out Winona Cobbs-Sanchez and her husband, Stanley, in a suit and tie.

Lucy waved to both of them. She was getting more and more agitated by the second. Every attraction that passed meant Little Cowpokes' parent-and-child march, their portion of the parade, was getting closer.

And then, there they were. Strollers, toddlers, three-

and four-year-olds. Coming toward her with their parents. All of them wearing the Little Cowpokes T-shirts identical to the one her mom had had on that morning. Angela and Elaina were both there, of course, in the middle of the crowd. Waving at everyone.

Lucy knew every single one of them. Had hugged every one of those children. She waved. Until her gaze lit on Noah, with his parents on each side of him, as he pushed Charlie, Henry and Gavin in the cutest-ever miniature hay wagon. At least based on the one side of it she caught in peripheral vision. She hadn't been going to look at the boys. Knew she'd cry if she did. But it turned out she didn't have enough self-control to follow her own mandate. And there they were. Pieces of her heart. In their parade T-shirts. Sitting in a row in that wagon. At a stop because Winona and Stanley were talking to someone at the curb beside their float.

She glanced up briefly, to see the holdup, but had to get right back to those three precious boys. And then, as though she had no mind of her own, glanced back at their father again. Recognizing everything about him. The stiff set of his broad shoulders that took on the entire world around him. The strained smile on his so-handsome face.

He'd had a haircut.

And she was so in love with the man she could hardly keep herself from calling out to him. She had to get out of there. Go home. Maybe come back after the picnic.

She took one step back, thinking she'd push her way through the people behind her, but froze when she saw Charlie stand up in the wagon. Noah reached for him, but Henry was standing, too, and then little Gav, and

Noah only had two hands. Olive was talking to one of the parents walking beside her. Someone on the opposite curb had called out to Christopher. Lucy saw it all in slow motion. Opened her mouth to scream, but saw Charlie reach the ground safely after his climb out of the wagon, and race straight toward her.

"MeWoo! MeWoo! MeWoo!" It was like the entire world stopped around them. Frozen frame. Just she and Charlie moved. Bending down, she held out her arms and the little one flew into them, his arms around her neck. "MeWoo at Fork Hoowee!"

As though he'd known she was coming.

Before she could do anything but bury her face against his neck, kissing him, she felt another very familiar pair of chubby toddler arms around one of her legs. "Wooo! Wooo!" Followed, a little further in the distance by "Ooo Ooo Ooo Ooo."

She pulled Henry in close and held on, and then glanced up to see Noah, with Gavin on his hip, arms outstretched toward her.

There was no way she could stop the tears from pooling in her eyes, so she didn't try. She blinked at them. Saw Olive and Christopher Trent standing a few feet in the distance as the parade moved on by without them. Both of them had warm expressions on their faces.

And the next moment's future became clear to Lucy.

Looking up at Noah, she had one thing to say.

"We need to talk."

Noah wasn't sure what he and Lucy had left to say to each other. He'd overheard Elaina telling another parent who'd asked that Lucy loved her new job with Washington Marketing, and that they were paying her more than she'd counted on. Clearly a proud mama moment.

One that had both pleased and devastated him at the same time. As though some irrational, untethered part of him had secretly been hoping that she'd hate Denver. Or find the new job opportunity similar to the one in Bronco that she'd turned down.

After the parade, he handed his three unhappy-to-be-leaving-Lucy munchkins over to his parents, and followed Lucy through the people thronging Central Avenue to a deserted alcove entrance to one of the closed businesses around the corner.

"How long are you in town for?" Noah blurted before she could say whatever it was she had to say. Some rendition of the "Thank you, you were right" message he was bracing to hear.

"For the rest of my life," she said, her chin raised, as though daring him to do anything but accept her words.

It took him a second to actually grasp their meaning. He'd been too busy trying to get them to sound like the ones he'd expected to hear.

"What? You have nothing to say to that?" she asked then. Not quite in a teasing tone, but not in an overtly nasty one, either.

"Why can't you ever just say what you feel, Noah?" she asked next.

He caught the frustration inherent in that one. But before he could respond, she was coming at him again.

"Don't you miss me? Don't you miss *us*?"

He had an answer. "Of course," he blurted, relieved to have something to contribute. To be able to get words past the constriction in his throat.

She was so passionate, so beautiful. So confident in ways he wasn't sure he ever had been. But he knew what he knew. "Your mom says you took the job. That you love it. Turns out you made the right decision to go."

And she'd just said she was back in town for good. Or had that answer just been a sarcastic taunt? He'd been too blindsided by the words to catch any nuances.

"You kind of made the decision for me, didn't you?" she asked. Her tone sounded...not good. But the look in her eyes as they met his—he recognized something there.

A warmth that was very good.

"I get that you're only trying to do what's best for your family, and for me, too, Noah. And I get why you're trying so hard to keep my needs in the mix. What you went through with Joanna...it was tragic. Eye-opening to say the least. Devastating. But while you're so busy trying to make sure you don't make the same kind of mistake again...you're sort of making it. You're seeing things from your viewpoint. Not mine. Which is all any of us can ever do, really. And that's why it's so important to listen. You aren't listening to my needs, Noah."

Feeling as though he only had seconds to save a life, Noah stared at her, couldn't look away. And had no idea how to make everything right.

"I'm younger than you are," Lucy said then, as though in the midst of one of those conversations where the obvious was stated. "And I haven't been through a difficult break up. But I've had other experiences, Noah. Ones pertinent to my life. Ones that you haven't had. I've lived outside of Tenacity, in the big city, for years. You've never lived off the Stargazer."

He nodded. Liked the point. "Go on." She'd told him to listen.

"It doesn't have to be either-or, Noah. I do like the new job a lot. It's challenging and exciting with all kinds of opportunities…"

What was she doing? Offering him hope, making him feel as though she was saving him from making the biggest mistake of his life, and then killing him all at once?

"But the job I love is the remote one. Training is done. And I'm home. I like my work, Noah, but I love my life in Tenacity."

Her life in Tenacity. Not him. No. He stopped the thought process. Because Lucy was right. Instead of listening to her, he'd been so busy trying not to miss anything about her, that he'd gone a step too far. Put himself into what he perceived her position to be. And by so doing, he'd done her thinking for her. Which was worse, or at least as bad as, not seeing her at all.

But there was more. A part that had no basis in nobility. Every time Lucy had managed to sneak past his defenses, he'd pushed her away.

You really being self-sacrificing here? Or just protecting that bruised heart of yours?

Ryder's words from earlier in the week came back to him.

Raising a hand to the side of his face, rubbing her thumb on his chin, Lucy said, "You've been looking at this the wrong way, Noah."

A conclusion he was reaching all by himself.

"Instead of thinking about what I might be giving up in a relationship with a divorced older man with triplets ready to go into their terrible twos, think about what I might be getting. I've never felt this way about another man, Noah. Keeping in mind that we discovered that I've had more experience in that area than you have. And what's far more important is that my heart and soul are telling me that I'm never going to feel this way again. You're a once-in-a-lifetime kind of love. And the boys. Sorry to break it to you, but there's nothing you can do about how much I love them. Whether I ever see them again or not, they are already my family."

Noah blinked at the moisture in his eyes. His throat clogged with emotion, and he couldn't look away from her. Couldn't imagine how he'd come to deserve her, either.

She held his gaze as the thoughts skidded their way through him.

"What are you thinking?" she asked softly.

The words were just there. "About how much I love you." And with their release, there was no going back. No holding back. Pulling her fully into the privacy of the alcove, and as hard against him as he could without hurting her, he took his first full breath since she'd left town and lowered his lips to hers.

With the first touch, he felt her hunger. On a scale that matched his own. By some grace of the powers watching over him, he retained enough rationality to realize they could be discovered at any moment, and though he couldn't let go of her, he raised his head.

"I'm so sorry for having our discussions all by myself," he said, holding her face with both hands as his was held by hers. And he promised, "From now on, I will let you in...all the way in. And I will always listen to you when it comes to your wants and needs." But he couldn't leave it there. He'd gone too far to stop. "And someday, when you're sure you're ready, I will ask you to marry me."

Grinning, Lucy touched the corner of his mouth with her thumb and said, "Well, if we're listening to my needs, nix the someday. I'm ready now, Noah. The sooner the better. Our boys are already two. I'd like the memories they hang on to as they grow to include me living in their home, not just visiting it." Her smile faded as she added, "Seriously? Where else do I belong? I'm too old to be living with my parents. And it seems... wrong... for me to buy that little house, when my family has a home already."

Noah's first instinct was to argue. To be reasonable. Sensible. Look for the possible pitfalls to her and his boys.

To hold himself back from what he wanted most. The thought hit him hard.

And in that moment, Noah forgave himself for the mistakes of his past, as Joanna had long ago done, so that he could be every good thing possible for the loved ones in his future. He would never forget what had been, nor should he. But he made a silent vow to the woman he loved and to his current and future children, that he would be forever present for them, with his heart and mind fully opened to their shared lives ahead. Whatever they turned out to be.

Knowing that no matter what hardships might present along the way, he and Lucy would get through them together.

Lucy floated through the rest of that day. And at the same time, every memory became engraved in her heart, to be forever remembered.

She and Noah went with Olive and Christopher to

the picnic. Elaina joined them for a time, with each of the three boys toddling over to give her a hug. And her mother pulled her aside long enough to say, "I was so wrong to doubt you, sweetie. Welcome home."

Giving her mom a big hug, Lucy said, "You might change your mind when I'm hitting you up for favors and advice every step of the way." But she knew Elaina never would change her mind. Just as she wasn't ever going to stop loving, caring for and wanting to be there for Charlie, Henry, Gavin, Noah and whatever future children fate might bestow upon their family.

Lucy insisted on leaving the celebrations after lunch so that the boys could have their naptime. And while both sets of grandparents, the biological and the new set of the heart, insisted that they could handle naps so that Lucy and Noah could join the fun, Lucy just shook her head.

And felt her heart soar as Noah said, "It's a mother's prerogative," and, with a boy in each arm, leaving Gavin for Lucy's hip, as always, walked their family to his truck.

A mother's prerogative. With her being the mother.

That was when she knew, for sure, that he understood. She wasn't just choosing to be with him. To share his family. She needed them, just as they needed her.

Not to take care of her. But to fill their rightful place in her heart.

That night, she was filled to overflowing, literally, with tears filling her eyes as she sat on a blanket on the grass at the base of the steps leading up to the cement platform stage in the park, waiting for opening remarks before the fireworks started.

"Fire. Ky." Charlie—who was standing beside her,

balancing himself with a hand on her shoulder—said. For at least the eighteenth time.

"In a minute, bud," she told him again. An equal number of times. And would continue telling him, as long as he needed the answer.

She caught a glance from both of her parents, on their blanket just to the right of them. Figured them for having been talking about her. In the best of ways. She smiled. They smiled back.

And she knew what being truly happy meant.

Realized that she'd recognized it when it hit her because she'd grown up in a home filled with it.

Olive and Christopher Trent were on a blanket just behind them. Ready to be backup in case the fireworks frightened any of the three boys and the others wanted to stay.

Just as she and Noah would be doing someday for their own grandkids. Right there in Tenacity, she hoped. With some of them living at the Stargazer.

Leaning over to Noah, who had Henry attempting to poke a finger up his nose, she said, "This is true wealth."

With his son's curious finger in hand, Noah leaned over and kissed her. Right there in front of the whole town.

Just as the lights up on the platform came on, to show Winona and Stanley, still in parade garb, standing together, holding hands. Each with a microphone in the other.

"Good evening, and welcome to Tenacity's annual Fourth of July fireworks celebration," Stanley started in.

And ninety-eight-year-old Winona lifted her microphone. "But before we begin, we have a brief piece of important business to share with you."

Stanley pulled his mic closer to his mouth and said,

"We, my beautiful bride and I, with the help of her well-known special powers, may have finally cracked the mystery of what happened here in town with the Deroy family and the missing money fifteen years ago."

Winona looked up at Stanley, and Lucy felt the love the two shared clear to her core. Because she was tapped into the exact same source. "Our discovery could be the first step on the path to healing Tenacity," the psychic said.

And her new husband added, "There will be a town meeting tomorrow to discuss."

Looking at Noah then, eyes wide, Lucy asked, "What do you think that's about?"

"I have no idea, but we need to be there."

She'd have said more, but at that moment, the first series of fireworks shot up into the sky, showering them with sprays of color, one after another, lighting the town.

And Lucy's whole world.

With Henry in her lap, and Charlie on his knees beside her, she glanced over to check on Gavin. Their youngest's gaze was serious, but with interest, not fright, as he studied the sky above them. Lucy raised her eyes to find Noah watching her, not the sky.

Leaning over he said, "I love you, Lucy Bernard, soon to be Lucy Trent."

"I love you, too, Noah," she got out before his lips covered hers.

"Fire ky!" Charlie said. "MeWoo Da ick."

Ick. Charlie's word for kiss.

And the seal of approval that made Lucy's heart whole.

* * * * *

Don't miss the next installment of the new continuity
Montana Mavericks: The Tenacity Social Club

Their Maverick Summer
by Christy Jeffries
On sale July 2025, wherever
Harlequin books and ebooks are sold.

And look for the previous books in the series,

The Maverick's Promise
by Melissa Senate

A Maverick's Road Home
by USA TODAY *bestselling author Catherine Mann*

All in with the Maverick
by Elizabeth Hrib

A Maverick Worth Waiting For
by USA TODAY *bestselling author Laurel Greer*

Available now!